The Cannon

The Cannon

Gholam-Hossein Sa'edi

Translated and Introduced
by
Faridoun Farrokh

Ibex Publishers,
Bethesda, Maryland

The Cannon by Gholam-Hossein Sa'edi
Translated and Introduced by Faridoun Farrokh
Translation Copyright © 2010 Faridoun Farrokh

Photograph of cannon on cover courtesy of Fauxto Digit.
Photograph of Sa'edi courtesy of Faridoun Farrokh.

ISBN-10: 1-58814-068-7
ISBN-13: 978-1-58814-068-5

All rights reserved. No part of this book may be reproduced or retransmitted in any manner whatsoever except in the form of a review, without permission from the publisher.
Manufactured in the United States of America
The paper used in this book meets the minimum requirements of the American National Standard for Information Services—Permanence of Paper for Printed Library Materials, ANSI Z39.48–1984

Ibex Publishers strives to create books which are as complete and free of errors as possible. Please help us with future editions by reporting any errors or suggestions for improvement to the address below, or corrections@ibexpub.com

Ibex Publishers, Inc.
Post Office Box 30087
Bethesda, Maryland 20824
Telephone: 301–718–8188
Facsimile: 301–907–8707
www.ibexpublishers.com

Library of Congress Cataloging-in-Publication Data
Sa'idi, Ghulam Husayn.
[Tup. English]
The cannon / by Gholam-Hossein Saedi ; translated and introduced by Faridoun Farrokh.
p. cm.
ISBN-13: 978-1-58814-068-5 (alk. paper)
ISBN-10: 1-58814-068-7 (alk. paper)
1. Iran—History—1905–1911—Fiction. I. Title.
PK6561.S27T813   2009
891'.5533—dc22   2009002228

TABLE OF CONTENTS

About the Text..6

Acknowledgments 7

Introduction..9

Works Cited...22

The Cannon...25

ABOUT THE TEXT

This translation is based on the original Persian text of *Tup*, published by Entesharat-e Agah, Tehran, 2536 (1977). Persian words and proper names in the text have not been transliterated for an academic audience, but have been rendered as they would best sound to the English reader. Glottal stops are symbolized by apostrophes.

ACKNOWLEDGMENTS

Despite trepidations as to my ability to do justice to Sa'edi's inimitable prose style, I pressed on with the project and brought it to fruition essentially thanks to the support and encouragement of my wife, Lucinda Farrokh, who gave me valuable advice on matters of idiom and expression, and M.R. Ghanoonparvar of the University of Texas at Austin, who took a vital interest in this endeavor and kept a benign eye on its progress.

I am also indebted to Farhad Shirzad, my editor at Ibex Publishers, who reviewed the manuscript with remarkable alacrity and made trenchant suggestions for its improvement. Any merits the readers may find in this translation is to a large measure due to these individuals. However, what there may be by way of flaws and infelicities are entirely my own.

Faridoun Farrokh,
September 2008,
Laredo, Texas

INTRODUCTION

In the early morning of Saturday, November 24, 1985, Gholam-Hossein Sa'edi died in a Paris hospital and with his death ended an era of intellectual and artistic development in Iran that was in various degrees marked by opposition to the oppressive nature of the Pahlavi régime, a resurgence of nationalism combined with cultural self-analysis, and a running battle with the influence of the West. Sa'edi, with more than forty works of fiction, non-fiction, and drama to his credit, himself was an embodiment of this spirit in the literary history of the period which had its beginning in the early years after the Second World War, culminating in the installation of clerical rule in 1978.

Sa'edi was born on January 5, 1936, in Tabriz to a middle-class family. Indications are that he received a sound education marked by extensive readings both in Persian and Western classics. Although his studies culminated in a medical degree from Tabriz University in 1960, during the years of his schooling Sa'edi participated in such literary activities as writing reviews and short fiction in local newspapers and magazines. He even published a short story in *Sokhan,* a highly respected literary publication in Tehran during his senior year in secondary school.

Soon after graduation from medical school he moved to Tehran where for two years he served in the armed forces in fulfillment of his national service following which he was awarded a residency in psychiatry in one of the major medical centers in Tehran. Despite the demands of medical training, Sa'edi persisted in his involvement in literary activities which included writing short stories and dramatic sketches one of which—a pantomime titled *Faghir* [The Mendicant]—was broadcast on the state television. It was during this period in his life that Sa'edi developed an interest in anthropological research. This prompted him to travel widely in the tribal areas in Azerbaijan Province and littoral plains of the Persian Gulf. He later published the results of his research in several treatises that proved controversial and incited much commentary pro and con. Later, he used some of his findings on the mechanics of intertribal relationships in the development of *Tup* [The Cannon], one of his three full-length novels.

From early on, Sa'edi identified himself with the dissent movement. In fact he was barely seventeen years old when he was first detained by the authorities for his activism as a student. Later in life he had numerous confrontations with the authorities and periods of incarceration in the sixties and seventies. This involvement has colored much of Sa'edi's output, which is frequently couched in conspicuously Iranian values and is intended to portray the pernicious effects of tyranny and oppression on society and the individual. While in his works, either drama or fiction, he subjected the salient features of the Iranian identity to rigorous scrutiny and trenchant criticism, his underlying intent was to voice, sometimes subtly but more often openly, objections to a mindless following of the Western mores and to expose the social and political ills of his country.

Despite his political activism and radical views on social change, Sa'edi never joined any organized group or party except for his membership in the Writers' Union. This organization, formed in 1968 by a handful of liberal-minded writers and intellectuals of diverse backgrounds and persuasions, later played a legendary role in concentrating the efforts of the Iranian intelligentsia against the Pahlavi rule in the years preceding the the 1979 revolution. Sa'edi's association with the Writers' Union proved very constructive and fruitful and gave him a platform from which he launched his literary career. It is obvious that

Introduction

early on Sa'edi had decided to deploy his considerable literary talent in the service of his philosophical ideals. Although later in life he became a medical doctor and specialized in psychiatry, he spent much of his time writing and in other literary activities, becoming an influential member of that coterie of literary men and women who came to be known as "committed" writers.

It has been generally noted, and succinctly put in Minoo Southgate's introduction to her English translation of Sa'edi's *Fear and Trembling*, that "since the classic genres [in Persian literature], being stylized and conventional in theme, vocabulary, and form, did not lend themselves to realistic portrayals of life, they were abandoned [by contemporary writers] in favor of new literary forms." Some Western forms, asserts Southgate, offered the desired versatility and they were, therefore, considered by Iranian writers for adoption (viii).

It was in this spirit, and not because of infatuation with the west, that Sa'edi immersed himself in a study of Western literature and history. In addition to the writers of the antiquity and classical periods, he studied such modern notables as Chekhov, Sartre, Apollinaire, Lorca, Borges, Brecht, Eliot and countless others (Southgate viii). He must have realized, given the vast scope of his reading, that more than any other literary genre, drama has been used as a platform from which to make statements of social and philosophical import. "Theater in the Theatrical Régime," a treatise vehemently critical of the Islamic rulers of Iran, is succinctly revealing of Sa'edi's profound understanding of the public impact of drama within body politic, an impact that goes far beyond the aesthetics of a literary work:

Perhaps many may think that a régime, a ruling order [meaning the Islamic Republic], given to histrionic antics, does not need the theater. But that is not the case. A theatrical régime makes a show not only of life's daily events or non-events, of its own presence on the seat of power, of the ancestral past, but also of the theater, this innocent, courageous, and sincere art form. A theatrical régime will not leave theater alone. It will find this worthless, discarded staff useful, and utilize it as a crutch. To prolong its political life, this régime grabs at everything, even its own enemy, the theater. (1)

Clearly, Sa'edi was cognizant of the fact that the nature of theatrical presentation is such that it lends itself to propagandistic purposes. As it unfolds upon the stage, the action projects a flesh-and-blood immediacy that involves the audience in the dynamics of a developing situation. However, the audience is simultaneously aware that the action as it unfolds on the stage is at a long remove from the events that inspired it. Providing that the play is well-conceived and well-written, and the action on the stage is skillfully performed, the characters become archetypes and the outcome of their external struggles and internal conflicts takes on the timelessness and potency of universal truths.

The influence exerted by the heritage of the classical Greek drama on the mainstream of western thought and culture is a case in point. Sa'edi was fully aware that in spite of its structural simplicity, the Greek drama developed as a highly sophisticated and intricate means to instill in audiences religious concepts and values which formed the ideological basis of its function. As the significance of its religious dimension faded, Greek drama served countless generations as a catalyst in the assimilation of the facts of life and a guide in the quest for spiritual self-knowledge. Its heroes, at crucial points in the course of the play, act on their own responsibility and refuse to be mere cogs in the great machinery of fate. In *Prometheus Bound*, for example, Prometheus knowingly assists Zeus in overcoming his father, Cronus, and establishing his ascendancy over the gods, and just

Introduction

as knowingly, and in deference to a higher purpose than self-interest, he antagonizes Zeus by endowing man with the gods' prerogative, the secret of fire. In *Antigone* there is nothing flagrant or self-indulgent in the protagonist's challenge to Creon. She makes a deliberate choice to uphold the divine law in opposition to Creon's man-made decree. The pain and indignity inflicted upon her, therefore, is not merely to arouse sympathy for the suffering of a martyr, but to promote in the audience a deep sense of the realities of life when it comes to making a choice in the matter of following the dictates of one's conscience. In most of his plays Sa'edi follows this pattern, infusing the same spirit into a relatively simple framework, and by so doing avoids mechanical exemplification and explicit highlighting of moral precepts which are the hallmarks of didactic and doctrinaire art and literature. And yet his style and technique are quite individual and it is not possible to attribute any aspect of his dramaturgy to any specific influence, classic or modern, native or foreign. In fact, in "BBC Radio Interview with Dr. Gholam-Hossein Sa'edi," when the reporter suggests that every writer is inspired and influenced by another, Sa'edi energetically rejects the notion and states: "Yes, I will kiss the hands, and feet, of Chekhov. He wrote the best plays. For me, Brecht is an extraordinary dramatist. But I think as long as an artist does not stand on his own two feet and has no faith in his own work and inspiration, he is exactly like the person, you know, who dreams of those 'inspiring angels' at night—and you know what a mess is the result of that!"

In encountering the structural simplicity of Sa'edi's plays, one is mindful of the cultural significance of that peculiarly Iranian Shiite religious ritual called the *ta'zyieh* and its possible influence on his dramatic works. The *ta'zyieh* is a variety of passion play presenting the persecution and martyrdom of Shiite heroes and saints. As Peter Chelkowski notes in his study of this cultural phenomenon, its similarities with the European medieval theater of the Stations of the Cross are striking (3). It is safe to assume that the parallelisms between *ta'zyieh* and its European counterparts did not escape Sa'edi's notice. Obviously such religiously inspired drama is intended to galvanize audiences and activate their zeal. As we know, after the entrenchment of the Christian church and the establishment of its rituals and ceremonies, dramatic representation was seized upon to augment the impact of periodic liturgy and facilitate the propagation of church doctrine. These aims were achieved by dramatizing the accounts of important religious occasions such as Easter or the martyrdom of saints. In England, the records of such dramatic or quasi-dramatic representation—often in Latin and devised by high-ranking clergy—go back to the tenth century. Medieval drama does not lend itself to close critical scrutiny and analytical study because the chronologies are often indeterminate and records fragmentary. Nevertheless, an evolutionary process can be observed in the appearance of more and more subtle and sophisticated forms of religious drama. They include pageants, mysteries, miracles, and interludes, the last of which spanned the transition period between the medieval religious drama and the professional theater which appeared with the building of playhouses and formation of acting companies. This process led eventually to the blooming of the dramatic arts in the age of Shakespeare and beyond.

In Iran, however, no such strong secular dramatic tradition had developed, despite the fact that, according to Chelkowski, "in the entire Muslim world, Persia was the only country to nourish drama" in the form of the *ta'zyieh* which took nearly a thousand years to develop. However, unlike its European counterpart, *ta'zyieh* was never secularized. "That this should be so," accord-

Introduction

ing to Chelkowski, "especially in view of Persia's close cultural and geographic ties with Greece and India, both of which had extraordinarily rich theatrical traditions, remains a puzzle" (4). Therefore, when Sa'edi began his career as a dramatist in the early sixties, he did so in an atmosphere by and large unfamiliar with the intricacies of modern drama. It is true that in Tehran and other population centers playhouses had existed, but they were mostly a venue for staging vaudeville and burlesque types of entertainment generally for the benefit of lower-class audiences. The only occasional smattering of legitimate theater had been productions of plays from European dramatists performed by amateurs often in association with the staffs of foreign embassies or under the auspices of bi-national societies. Sa'edi's plays (published under the pseudonym Gowhar Morad and some in the form of one-act dramatic sketches), too, were at first produced and viewed by small groups of university students as "theatrical experiments" and it was not until the early seventies that they received wider audiences.

His earliest known full-length play formally produced on the stage, *Workaholics in Trenches* (1960), is constructed around the problems arising from rapid industrialization in a rural community somewhere in southern Iran. The theme of the play is not original—in the sense that it involves issues resulting from the confrontation of the old and the new—and it becomes somewhat hazy because the plot is overwrought and complex. Jalal Minu, a young engineer, operates a sulfur-extracting plant somewhere in the coastal region of the Persian Gulf. He faces problems inherent in the collision of the old and the new. Local landowners and gentility view the plant and its operation detrimental to the established patterns of economic production and likely to shift the balance of political power in the area. Naturally, they cause problems for the young engineers and try to derail the operation of the plant. But that is only a part of Minu's problem; because he is totally absorbed in the management of the plant, his wife becomes increasingly alienated from him and teeters on the verge of mental and emotional collapse. Later, when he tries to help an old friend, who hides from him his illegal activities in the recent past, Minu is implicated in an unlawful enterprise leading to his arrest and the loss of his reputation.

The conventionality of the theme and the multi-layered plot of *Workaholics* has been attributed by one commentator to the fact that this is one of Sa'edi's earliest works and it displays insecurity in his approach to the genre. According to Abdol 'Ali Dastghayb, "the organization of the play lacks the necessary cohesiveness." Dastghayb feels that the character of Minu is underdeveloped. He is presented as a highly educated and successful entrepreneur and yet, implausibly, he is shown to be incapable of defending himself against false charges. His attempt in the final scene to effect an escape to avoid arrest by the gendarmes is out of character and unaccountable. Dastghayb postulates that Sa'edi had meant to bestow the character of Minu with the nobility of a tragic hero but has not been wholly successful. Still, Dastghayb praises Sa'edi for his success in depicting the texture of the relationship between Minu and his wife. "Their close unison at the beginning of married life," he notes, "has now dissolved and they are drifting so far apart that there is no understanding between them." He further notes that the importance of this play, given its political and social context, is in its attention to the daily social events and introduction of a host of new personages into the cast of characters. In addition, states Dastghayb, "Sa'edi pursues social problems more assiduously [than other playwrights of the period] and demonstrates the liberal and progressive approach … in depicting the trans-

Introduction

mutations taking places in the deep recesses of society" (74-75). These "transmutations" are identified by M.R. Ghanoonparvar who notes that in *Workaholics* "the focus is on the conflicts that ensue as a result of rapid industrialization." To demonstrate the ramifications of this phenomenon, Ghanoonparvar writes:

Both the plot and subplot [of the play] address the dilemmas confronted by the society: on one level, the dilemma of industrial progress versus the traditional economic structure and, on the other, the dilemma of the breakdown of family and individual relationships as a result of changes in the value system and the importance placed on progress at any cost (xxi).

Later in his career, Sa'edi moved progressively toward more austere forms of dramatic expression with terser, more pointed social content. A representative specimen is *Chub beh Dasthaye Varazil* [The Club-Wielders of Varazil] (1965). In this play one of the denizens of the village of Varazil, Moharam, whose crops have been decimated by a boar and is beset by financial ruin, is alienated from his fellow-villagers because he scorns their reliance on their clubs against the ravages of wild animals. This undermines the villagers' confidence in their own ways of defending their crops and they seek help from outsiders, in this case a "consultant" presumably of foreign descent. The "consultant" sends two hunters armed with rifles, suggesting their technological ascendancy over the villagers. Although they seem to deflect the boars initially, themselves soon become a burden on the village by their rapacity and slothfulness. Further appeals to the consultant leads to the dispatch of additional hunters who immediately join forces with the first group in exploiting the villagers. Ultimately, the people of Varazil arrive at the conclusion that they should themselves address their problems rather seek the assistance of venal, self-interested outsiders. Using their clubs, they expel the venal outsiders from their village. To communicate the subversive thrust of the play, which contains not only an overall statement about the exploitation of the third world by the West but also a sharp criticism of the Shah's foreign policy at the time, Sa'edi has devised a complex symbolic structure, in which almost all elements of the play—characters, scenes, props, and even lighting—conveys a message beyond what it denotes. The dialogue is designed to lend itself to modification by local accents and dialects, a quality which has made the play accessible to audiences of various levels of intellectual sophistication. A prominent critic, Najaf Daryabandari, faults the play on weaknesses in its developmental patterns of the plot and some disjuncture between acts one and two. While he finds that first act satisfactorily sets up the theme and functional dynamics of the play, the second act fails to rise to the expectations promoted in the audience (489-490). "Nevertheless," he points out, "these should not prevent us from admiring Mr. Sa'edi's originality in entertaining us with a serious work of drama. Let us agree that the success of the first act is the success of the entire play" (491).

As a whole, Sa'edi used the same technique in most of the plays that he wrote in the middle years of his career. The result is such popular plays as *Panj Nemayeshnameh as Enghelab-e Mashrutyyat* [Five Sketches on the Constitutional Revolution] (1966), *Dikteh va Zavyyeh* [Dictation and Angle], published in tandem (1968), and *Parvar Bandan* [Cattle Fatteners] (1969). In later years, however, he turned to more specific issues and made more vociferous objections to the intimidation of the citizenry and emasculation of political opposition. During this period Sa'edi's plays display a more rigid structure with characters more realistically conceived. A representative play is *Mah-e Asal* [The Honeymoon] (1978). Set against the background of an apartment in a city such as Tehran, the play is manifestly a slice of

Introduction

urban life. A newly-wed couple, clearly in love, are caught in a web of intrigue insinuated by a matronly woman placed in their apartment by a government ordinance. Due to their youth and concomitant immaturity, the couple fall victim to the machinations of the old and become alienated from each other, turning into "non-thinking machine-like creatures whose only concern is eating and drinking." (Southgate xv). In this play "Sa'edi presents a society being totally brainwashed and controlled by its governing apparatus," asserts M.R. Ghanoonparvar, who believes that *The Honeymoon* "is an allegory of Iran in the 1970's when the Shah with his SAVAK ... appeared to many people to have created a police state, with spies seeming to infiltrate all aspects of Iranian life, public and private" (xxii).

* * *

It is true that Sa'edi's literary reputation rests principally on his dramatic works, but he produced a significant body of fiction that stands on its own in literary and artistic merit. Most of his short stories were collected and published in *Azadaran-e Bayal* [The Mourners of Bayal] (1964), *Vahemeha-ye bi nam va neshan* [Nameless and Elusive Apprehension] (1966), and *Dandil* (1966). More so than his plays, according to Dastghayb, his fiction is reflective of his training as a psychopathologist. He finds that Sa'edi's fiction is different from that of other contemporary writers with a psychological bent in that he relates the psychosis of his characters to social conditions rather than individual dispositions and temperaments (11-12). A notable case in point is a short story title "Gav" [The Cow] which appeared in *Azadaran-e Bayal*. The story is focused on a villager whose cow, the only source of his livelihood and a symbol of his status in the impoverished village, dies. The event proves devastating to the villager not only from a material point of view but also because of sentimental attachment to the animal. As a result, he succumbs to a psychotic state of personality disorder imagining himself to be the cow. Sa'edi poignantly traces the process and adds a touch of irony when the village community after an interval begins to treat him as a cow.

Soon after its appearance, "The Cow" caught the attention of Dariush Mehrjui, at the time a young and promising film director, who in cooperation with Sa'edi made it into a film. Appearing on the screen in the summer of 1969, "The Cow," skillfully and sensitively directed by Mehrjui and superbly acted by leading actors in the Iranian cinema, became a huge box-office success both in Iran and abroad.

* * *

By early 1970s Sa'edi had published a short novel, *Tup* [The Cannon] and completed the manuscripts of two more, *Gharibeh dar shahr* [Stranger in Town] and *Tatar-e Khandan* [Laughing Tartar]. The latter two were not published until 1990 and 1994 respectively due to the explicit criticism they leveled at the Pahlavi rule. In fact the first draft of *Tatar-e Khandan* was completed while Sa'edi was in detention.

The Cannon is set in the tribal region of northwestern Iran during the Iranian Constitutional Revolution from 1906 to 1910. The story follows the movements of a Cossack regiment of the czarist Russian army dispatched to the area to ward off the advances of the Constitutionalists against the central government in Tehran and counter their recruitment efforts among the tribes. At the center of the story is an itinerant cleric, Mullah Mir Hashem, who tends to the religious needs of the Shahsevan cluster of tribes. Throughout the years that the mullah has been pursuing his calling, or plying his trade, he has amassed a small fortune in the form of flocks of sheep that he

Introduction

entrusts for their care to the tribal shepherds. Now, the presence of foreign troops in the region and the distinct possibility of a clash with the tribes are likely to decimate his flocks and leave him penniless. The massive field gun that the Cossacks haul with them in their meanderings over the landscape, has struck an almost metaphysical fear in the mullah's heart and, to him, it has become an omen of ill fortune. The plot outlines the mullah's attempts to avert disaster by playing one side against the other. His ineptitude ultimately exposes his disingenuous disposition and spells his doom.

Despite the centrality of the mullah's role, the novel is not merely about him. There are other characters that display intriguing complexity and absorb our attention as they try to cope with the various dimensions of a clear and present danger. Among them are some tribal leaders and, of special interest, General Dolmachev, the commander of the Cossack regiment. As such, the story does not have a protagonist per se and may be described as a loosely structured series of scenes each with its own main character and its own focus. Sa'edi's triumph is in making these focal points yield a continuing story line culminating in a dramatic and surprising climax.

WORKS CITED

Chelkowski, Peter J. "Ta'ziyeh: Indigenous Avant-Garde Theatre of Iran." *Ta'ziyeh:*

Ritual and Drama in Iran. Ed. Peter Chelkowski. New York: New York University Press, 1979.

Daryabandari, Najaf. "A Glance at *Chub beh Dasthaye Varazil* [The Club-Wielders of Varazil] in *Introduction to Gholam-Hossein Sa'edi.* Ed. Javad Mojabi. Tehran: Nashr-e Atieh, 1999.

Dastghayb, Abdol 'Ali. *Naghd-e Asar-e Gholam-Hossein Sa'edi* [A Critique of the Works of Gholam-Hossein Sa'edi]. Teheran: Entesharat Chapar, 1973.

Ghanoonparvar, M.R. *Iranian Drama: An Anthology.* Costa Mesa, California: Mazda Publishers, 1989.

Sa'edi, Gholam-Hossein. Interview with BBC Reporter. *Sohabat-e Ahl-e Nazar.* (n.d.) Printed in *Alefba.* No. 7, 1986.

———. "Theater in the Theatrical Régime." *Alefba.* No. 5, 1984.

Southgate, Minoo. Introduction. *Fear and Trembling.* by Gholam-Hossein Sa'edi. Trans. Minoo Southgate. Washington DC: Three Continents Press, 1984.

The Cannon

ONE

In the morning they hauled the cannon up the hill and secured it on the emplacement they had built the day before. The gun now had the whole valley within range. Below its long barrel a narrow path wound around the hill. Sunlight was slowly spreading on the dew-laden vegetation of the valley floor, and the hills, like so many camels resting and ruminating, had turned their humps to the hazy morning light.

Four Cossacks, who had helped in pulling the cannon up the hill, were leaning against its carriage. The valley was bare and deserted except for a lonely tree among the hillocks, making nonchalant movements in the breeze.

A while later, Dolmachev, heavily bearded and covered in dust, came up the hill followed by the gunner. The Cossacks took note and moved away from the cannon.

Dolmachev first cast a sweeping glance over the valley and then fixed his gaze on the cannon, which was set amidst some boulders. He looked at the squat figure of the gunner who, still out of breath with the effort of hill climbing, was stroking the gleaming barrel of the huge artillery piece.

"Is it positioned right?" asked Dolmachev.

"Absolutely," snorted the gunner, laughing pointlessly.

The sun was now coming up, shortening the shadows and creating a faint rainbow in the thick morning mist on the brow of the neighboring hills.

Dolmachev turned around and viewed the Cossack encampment nestled at the backside of the hill in expectant silence. He then looked casually at the Cossacks near the cannon. Sheepishly, they stepped forward and stood at attention. Dolmachev ignored them and turned to the gunner.

"Are you all set?"

"As ever," said the gunner with a laugh.

"Are you sure?" Dolmachev asked.

"I'm sure I'm sure," chortled the gunner.

"Do you know the enemy?"

"Of course I do."

"I mean the real one."

"I know him."

"Who is the real enemy?"

"The first one who puts in an appearance around here," said the gunner snickering. This time Dolmachev also laughed and asked: "Will you fire?"

"Of course I will!"

"Wasting a round on one person?"

As he stroked the barrel of the cannon, the gunner said diffidently, "Not for one person. But if they are a bunch … of course."

A large dog came up the hill from the camp area. Dolmachev whistled and the dog sidled up to him and stopped by the gun. The gunner and the Cossacks were standing around taking in the fresh morning air.

After a few minutes, the dog cocked its ears and sprinted forward. "What's the matter?" said Dolmachev with alarm. The Cossacks cowered in readiness and the gunner jumped behind the cannon. Under his breath Dolmachev whispered, "The enemy. The real enemy." He turned to the gunner and said, "Ready!"

Below the hill, round the bend of the pathway, a lean and tall mullah on a horse came into view and as he cantered past the gun position unaware, Dolmachev whispered to the gunner, "Wait."

The Cannon

The gunner and the Cossacks remained motionless and watched as the mullah disappeared behind the hill. Dolmachev held the dog back so it would not bark.

"The real enemy just slipped through our fingers!" said the gunner in an attempt at humor. Except for him, nobody laughed.

TWO

It was past midnight when the mullah entered Movil from a side road. Through a narrow street crowded with clusters of trees he rode his way past three silent flourmills into the village square. The houses were unusually dark and quiet in the chilly, moist air of late summer. From a distance outside the village, he could hear an occasional bark of a dog. Confused and disoriented, the mullah looked around the square. He had never seen Movil so dark and silent. There was no sign of life anywhere. As he contemplated the unaccustomed silence, the horse, as on many other occasions, turned into the first alley which had a sizable opening and was flanked with tall adobe walls. The walls became lower and there were occasional chinks and cracks in them as the horse and rider went past small but heavy doors recessed into the walls. In front of the village alderman's compound the horse stopped and the mullah got off. The dwelling was dark and the door was well-buttressed, unyielding to pressure. With the chain he held in his hand, the mullah rapped on the door. A muffled bark of a dog was heard from inside. The mullah rapped the door harder and the dog stopped barking. Soon, the door was opened ajar and a man jutted his head out. He stared at the mullah for a short moment and blurted, "hey, Mullah! Is it you?"

"Greetings, Alderman," said the mullah. "Has something happened? Movil is deathly quiet."

As he opened the door, the alderman said, "Come on in. Movil has been deserted."

"Deserted?" gasped the mullah.

The alderman secured the door firmly with a piece of lumber and said, "Be quiet. Come on in."

The Cannon

The mullah, holding the bridle in his fist, stepped into the darkness. The horse resisted a moment before following the mullah into the passageway. The alderman took the bridle from the mullah and hitched the horse in the corner of a small backyard. The horse stuck its head in the manger that was close by.

Through the darkness the two men felt their way over some wet fodder and hay stepping into a fairly large, square yard faintly lit by the moon peeping over the hill. They passed in the shadows by the flower bed and entered a hall. The alderman held the mullah's hand as he led him into a den in which an oil lamp burned in an earthen jar.

The mullah placed his cape and saddle bag on the floor and sat close to the dug-out bread oven which radiated a pleasant warmth. The other man brought a water jug and some bread wrapped in cloth and placed them in front of the mullah. He then sat across from the mullah on the other side of the oven.

"Very well, Alderman, what has happened to Movil?" asked the mullah impatiently.

"Movil is no good anymore, Mullah."

"What is the matter?"

"Don't you see? It's been abandoned," said the alderman dejectedly. "We were always grateful that the village was not on the tribal migration path. Now we are caught in a bigger catastrophe."

The mullah, obviously flustered, said, "I don't follow, Alderman. Tell me pure and simple what has happened?"

"First have a bite to eat and rest. Then I'll tell you all about it," said the alderman.

The mullah unwrapped the cloth and, helping himself to some bread and cheese, said, "I am not tired. An hour ago I stopped for prayer and a bit of rest. Now tell me all about it."

"I don't know how to begin," said the alderman. "It's now been ten days since Movil's been in this situation. People just drove their cattle out of here and went to the caverns."

"Why the caverns?" asked the mullah.

The alderman said in a whisper, "A whole bunch of Cossacks have come into the summer camp area."

The mullah, his mouth stuffed, said with alarm, "Cossacks? When did they come?"

"It's been more than a week."

The mullah swallowed the un-chewed mouthful and asked, "Whereabouts are they now, Alderman?"

"They went through here and headed for Salavat Pass."

"Did you see them?"

"Of course I did. Everybody did."

"They have come to do what?" asked the mullah, looking confused.

"To put down the tribes," the alderman said reflectively, "That is, they have come to help Rahim Khan. With them they have a huge gun—God knows for what. They say it can wipe out a whole tribe with one shot."

"Mercy O Absent Imam!" intoned the mullah, openly disturbed.

"But they say," added the alderman, "that their general has sent word to Rahim Khan to go see him and Rahim Khan has got his nose out of joint and said that he does not need any help and is not going to see the general."

"What has the general said?"

"Nothing, really. There's been much talk back and forth and Rahim Khan has told the general to get lost or he will rout him. The general is pissed off. So he's ordered the gun to be deployed on top of the hill at Salavat Pass."

""Oh mercy," said the mullah, visibly distressed. "Let me see, Alderman, which tribe is near Salavat Pass?"

"Alarlu." he replied.

"Oh my God!" exploded the mullah. "I am ruined!" He then rose to his feet and started pacing so vigorously that turbulence from his robe almost put out the oil lamp.

The alderman, baffled by his reaction, asked, "Why are you doing this, Mullah?"

The mullah sat down, took off his turban and unbuttoned his shirt. "If something happens I'll be ruined," he said, oblivious to the other man. "Oh, the Wielder of the Zolfaqar*, I leave myself in your hands!" He got up again and resumed pacing nervously. The alderman stood up with his arms open in a protective gesture lest in his agitation the mullah should slip and fall into the oven. The mullah turned to him and said pleadingly: "Think of something, Alderman. What am I going to do?"

"What can we do, Mullah. It's all up to God."

"Don't say that, man. If they fall into the Cossacks' hands, whatever I have will be gone and I'll be ruined."

"You mean the Alarlus?" asked the alderman.

"It doesn't matter. Whichever tribe. I don't know how to put it, how to make you understand. You see, everything I have is with the tribes. What the hell am I going to do?" said the mullah, now beside himself with despair.

---

* An invocation of Ali, the first Imam in Shiite tradition and the fourth Caliph in Sunii tradition. "Zolfaqar" is the name of his double-edged scimitar.

"Firstly, God is merciful," said the alderman reassuringly. "God willing, nothing will happen. Secondly, even if no one else knows, the two of us know very well what havoc have the tribal folks wreaked upon the poor, unfortunate peasants. Generation after generation they have plundered the farmers. And now if anything happens to them, it is only just and what they have brought upon themselves. They have done something for which they have to pay penance. You and I are not involved. Besides, what difference is it going to make to you? If there are no more tribes tomorrow, you can still run your life and business in any village or town around. What are you worried about?"

The mullah squatted on the floor and turned to the alderman. "Now that things have come to this pass," he told him, "sit down and listen carefully."

The alderman slowly lowered himself to the floor looking at the mullah intently.

"In the last twenty some odd years," said the mullah, "I have ranged the heath and holt around here and have gotten to know every one and every place and everyone's gotten to know me too—very well, indeed." He then rattled off the names of the clans in the region. "And I'm welcome wherever I go." he went on. "After a lifetime of service and reciting the laments of the Martyrs among them, I have five or six hundred sheep with each tribe. In fact with the Hajjikhujalus alone I have twenty-four shepherds tending my flock. Don't judge me by my cap and slippers. If the tribes are routed, my back would be broken."

The alderman, his eyes wide with disbelief, said, "You're kidding, Mullah!"

"I swear to the Holiness of God. Why should I lie about something like that?" shouted the mullah.

"And until now you never let anybody know, Mullah?"

"What's the point? People will misunderstand and say that Mullah Mir Hashem has lined his pocket with the laments of the Imams. But now things have changed and I sure as hell don't know what to do."

"Where were you going before you stopped by?" asked the alderman.

"I was on my way to Moqanlu summer camp. Someone has passed away and I was going for the funeral. But I am not going there now."

"So what do you want to do?"

"I'm going to warn the clans not to go by Salavat Pass."

"Which way should they go, then?" fretted the alderman. "If the clans run into each other, there's going to be trouble. If they go by the mountain ridge, they'll run out of water."

"I'm not thinking of these things, Alderman," said the mullah. "Perhaps they won't run into each other if they detour, or run dry if they take the mountain ridge. But if they come within range of the Cossacks, that's the end of it all. Finished." He then jumped up and started gathering his things.

"What are you doing?" asked the alderman.

"I must get going," said the mullah resolutely.

"It's no use to leave at this time of the night," insisted the alderman. "Do you realize what kind of terrain you have to cover?"

"Yes, I know, I know," said the mullah irritably.

"It is very dangerous. You can't get a dog to leave the kennel this time of night. How do you dare head out into the wilderness?

"God is merciful," said the mullah. "Don't think about it."

"Stay overnight and get some rest," said the alderman. "I'll wake you up with the morning prayer call so you can get on your way."

"It's still early. Do you think I can sleep?"

"May God protect you," said the alderman.

The mullah carried his cape and saddlebag as he followed his host through the dark room into the relative brightness of the yard. The moon had left its perch atop the hill and was now in the middle of the sky. The villager picked up a bucket of water from the rim of the well, and when they entered the backyard he watered the horse. The mullah pushed the door wide open and stepped into the alley, followed by the alderman and the horse.

"Hey, Alderman," said the mullah, "I swear you to the Martyr of Karbala[*] not to talk to anyone about this matter."

"Don't worry," responded the alderman. "God speed."

The mullah mounted his horse. The animal, cautiously and deliberately, started to negotiate the steep descent down the alley. The other man climbed on a broken wall nearby and listened intently to the echo of the horse's footfalls booming in the hushed silence, drowning every other sound in the night for miles around.

---

[*] Hossein, the third Imam in the Shiite tradition, martyred at Karbala in 669 AD.

THREE

At the crack of dawn the mullah arrived in Takdam. Just outside the village he saw four men who were skinning a dead horse. Around them were dozens of buzzards with long featherless necks waiting in anticipation. The smell of the carcass had driven them to distraction; they were bouncing up and down and making strange noises. As the mullah approached, the men stopped and greeted him.

"What's happened?" the mullah asked.

"It dropped dead last night," said one of the men. "We are skinning it."

"If it died and was not properly slaughtered, its skin is no good. It's unclean," the mullah advised them.

Another one of the men chuckled and said, "The knife got to it in time." He then turned and pointed to a gaping slash at the horse's throat where the whiteness of the severed trachea shone in a mass of dark, curdled blood. The mullah noticed a large-toothed saw a few feet away.

Suddenly the mullah's horse lurched forward and set its legs apart and lowered its head. One of the men shouted "Hey, hey!" Hurriedly, the men who had pointed to the slit throat of the dead horse threw a dirty gunnysack over the wound. The mullah's horse gave a shudder and stood motionless and the men yelled "hey, hey" at the horse to distract it.

The first man turned to the mullah and said, "What a surprise to see you around here, Mullah."

"I am coming from Movil," said the mullah.

"I hope you're going to stay with us a few days," said one of the men.

"Just passing through," said the mullah laconically.

"On your way to the tribes?"

"No, to Salavat Pass."

"What have you got to do there?"

"Some business."

The men looked at one another for a brief moment and the one who had thrown the sack on the dead horse's neck said: "Haven't you heard?"

"Haven't heard what?" asked the mullah.

"That area is out of bounds. The Cossacks have occupied the Pass," said the man.

"Just yesterday I passed through and I didn't see anything," said the mullah.

"What are you talking about? Lots of Cossacks are over there," said another one of the men.

"Have you seen them yourselves?" asked the mullah.

"We haven't seen them," said the man with the knife, "but Baba has."

"Actually, he ran into them," interrupted the second man. "He had a hell of a time trying to get them to let him go."

"They thought he was a tribesman," resumed the first man, "and they were going to cut off his ears. He pleaded with them and swore that he was not. They let him go after they were convinced that he was the miller in this village."

"Where is he now?" enquired the mullah.

"Who?" asked the second man.

"He means Baba, of course," the first man told him. He then turned to the mullah and said: "He is at the mill."

"I'd better go see him," pondered the mullah. "May God be with you."

The Cannon

The men said nothing as the mullah turned his horse around and headed back. But after a few paces he stopped and turned to the men to get direction. One of them said, "Take the upper road. It's closer."

The mullah took a path that separated the village residences from the orchards and after skirting a hill the mullah came upon the ancient mill house that looked like a large bail of cotton among some old chestnut trees. The soft murmur of a rushing stream could be heard nearby.

The mullah dismounted and was looking around when Baba emerged from the house. The mullah greeted him. Baba approached with a look of disbelief on his face. "Blessed be your Grandsire, mullah. When did you get to Takdam?" he asked.

"Just now," replied the mullah

"Were you on the road through the night?"

"I was."

As he hitched the mullah's horse to a tree, Baba asked, "Were you by yourself?"

"Sure, Baba."

"God's been real merciful to you," said Baba with relief. "Don't you know what's going on?"

"I've heard the Cossacks are in the area," replied the mullah.

"What are you talking about, son, the world has turned upside down." said Baba, sounding quite distressed. "Everybody is at everybody else's throat! The Ghujabeyglus with the Hajjikhujalus, the Hajjikhujalus with the Alarlus, and the Alarlus with both of them. For his part, Rahim Khan has set fire to the world! He has ordered his riflemen not to take pity on anyone, young or old. He's told them to plunder the Shahsevans *and* the

Tots.* Now, everything aside," said Baba breathlessly, "the damned Cossacks too have joined the fray."

The two men passed through a low doorway and entered the millhouse, which was still murky in the faint morning light that streamed in through two small facing windows. A pile of empty flour sacks was stacked on the loading dock and everything was covered under the fine flour dust. The mullah and Baba plumped themselves down on a low platform near the door. The screeching of scurrying mice could easily be heard everywhere.

"It's all the fault of the government," said the mullah. "Since it is afraid that the tribes may go against it and join the Constitutionalists, it has lit this fire to divert their attention. May God have mercy on the Muslim folks."

"Doomsday is at hand and dogs don't know their masters any more," added Baba in confirmation.

"Bless you Baba, could you give me some water?" said the mullah. Baba reached under the platform and produced a jug of water and some bread wrapped in a bundle. He poured the water in a cup and handed it to him. The mullah drank most of the water and splashed the rest on his face. Baba unwrapped the bread and the two men started eating it with yogurt.

"I heard you had a run-in with the Cossacks," said the mullah.

"It was but for the grace of God that I was able to get away," replied Baba. "They were just about to do away with me."

"Now tell me all about it," the mullah urged him. "What did you say? What did you hear?"

"I was on my way to Hazan," Baba related, "when I ran smack into them. How can I tell you so you can imagine it? It was a sea

---

* Shahsevans are an ethnically and culturally homogenous group of clans settled by the Safavids in the northwestern plains of contemporary Iran in late 16th century. Most clans and tribes mentioned in this novel are Shahsevans. Tots, on the other hand, are presumably of Kurdish origin, indigenous to the region.

The Cannon

of soldiers. Row after row of tents. I was riding through the valley minding my own business when all of a sudden four wolf dogs set upon me. At first I thought they were from the tribes, but then I noticed the wide collars they were wearing. I lifted my legs up and pulled hard on the bridle to keep steady. Suddenly four sinister-looking Cossacks pounced upon me and dragged me over the hill. It was there that I saw the whole encampment. They were all lying around sunning themselves and staring at me. Then they took me to their general who was in his regimentals, sitting under a white canopy surrounded by a pack of dogs each the size of a donkey. He looked me over and asked which tribe I was from. None, I said. He frowned at me quietly and, I swear, so did his dogs, as if they understood human speech. He said again, 'Which Shahsevan are you?' and I said, 'I swear to the Holy Abbas* I am not a tribesman.' And then he said, 'Maybe whipping will jolt your memory,' and swore some curses in Russian under his breath. I said, 'I know you don't believe in an oath on the Holy Abbas. So why don't you send someone to Takdam to ask where I come from, to ask where this poor, miserable Baba works.' He just stared at me for a while and then chuckled. The dogs turned and looked at him. Then he told his men to let me go, which they did. I left with my heart way down in my boots and I got here I don't remember how."

"What about the cannon people are talking about?" said the mullah. "Is it a lie?"

"What?" exploded Baba. "A lie? I swear to the Holiness of God, I saw a cannon that no mortal can imagine. I just don't know how to describe it so you'd believe." He looked around the room in search of a basis for comparison, and not finding one, in exasperation said to the mullah, "come on, come on out. I'll

---

* A cousin of Imam Hussein, also slain at Karbala, hence a Shiite saint.

tell you." He led the mullah out of the house by the hand through the chestnut trees and swung him around. "Look," he said to the mullah. "You see the millhouse? The gun that I saw was twice the size of this building, like a mountain on two wheels. Its barrel went on and on all the way to the sky. Its mouth was so wide that you could easily throw a child into it. It was parked next to the hill and some Cossacks were building a platform for it halfway up the hill. The gunner was a ruddy-faced fellow with a neck as thick as a bull's. It looked like blood dripped from the tips of his mustache."

"Do you mean to say it is bigger than Rahim Khan's cannon?" asked the mullah.

"What are you talking about," chortled Baba disdainfully. If Rahim Khan's cannon be a canary, the general's is a camel!"

The mullah, overcome with awe, took a step backward and said, "Oh God the Merciful! Help me."

"I just can't figure out why they have brought it here," said Baba, thinking. "This thing can knock down a whole town let alone a dismal bunch of beggarly tribesmen."

"What am I to do?" the mullah whined.

"What are you to do?" said Baba, perplexed.

"May God bless your dead, Baba," pleaded the mullah. "Kindly get me a sack of bread, will you?"

Baba disappeared inside the mill house and the mullah, as he continued to take backward steps, saw the dilapidated building begin to grow in size and change its shape slowly and inexorably into the contours of a monstrous cannon.

FOUR

Inside a very large and black tent, in an armchair strewn with sheepskin sat Dolmachev, surrounded by a dozen or so oversized dogs with metal bands around their necks, lying lethargically around him.

Dolmachev, with his left foot resting lightly on the head of a dog, was stroking his beard pensively. From a vent on the topside of the tent the sun had cast a large golden circle on the floor near Dolmachev's foot. A black, short-haired dog had extended its paws in the sunlight and, with its head resting on its forelegs, was watching Dolmachev with drowsy eyes. Dolmachev, heavily bearded and with thick dark eyebrows, had an uncanny resemblance to his companions. But his round, protruding belly and clean, crisply pressed uniform gave him a regal air.

From inside the camp an occasional ripple of laughter or the sound of soldiers' horseplay was faintly audible. Dolmachev, still deep in thought, reached for a rope hanging over his head and gave it a tug. The sound of a bell reverberated outside. Presently, a short, dapper orderly stepped into the tent.

"Call Rahim Oghlu," ordered Dolmachev.

The orderly disappeared, wordlessly.

Within a few moments, a tall, broad-shouldered cossack entered the tent and stood at attention.

"Hey boy," barked Dolmachev, "how long do I have to stay here?"

"For as long as it is your pleasure, sir," demurred the cossack.

"Remember, I am not used to sitting in ambush like a cat," admonished Dolmachev. "I get bored."

"Whatever you say, Sir."

"I just want to get down to business as soon as possible."

"What can we do, Sir? We don't know the lie of the land."

"Get a-hold of a scout."

"There aren't any, sir."

"What about the farmers?"

"They are not familiar with the territory."

"I don't understand these things," yelled Dolmachev with irritation. "Find a scout. I don't care if you have to hire one or give him something."

Rahim Oghlu lowered his head in obedience and stepped out of the tent. The black dog lazily lifted itself up, put its front legs on the arm of the chair and lapped Dolmachev's large, corpulent hands.

FIVE

When he reached the top of the hill, a small summer camp spread before him on the other side. The sun was at its zenith and the meadow wore the faint orange tinge of the mid-day sun. No noise could be heard except the soundless breathing of the grass, or the distant gurgle of water being poured from a jug somewhere, an unseen bird winging in flight, a sheep bleating down the hill.

The mullah gave a sigh of relief and let the horse find its way down the steep hill. The animal was instinctively cautious. It would not lift a foot unless the other ones were secure on the downward path.

Half-way down the hill the light refracted and space appeared more open. The sheep, leaning against each other in tight flocks were resting on the grass. Tribal tents, in all sizes and shapes, extended beyond the meadow.

The mullah thought to himself that if it hadn't been the middle of the day, he could have seen smoke rising from kitchens preparing dinner. As the mullah got to the foot of the hill he heard a dog barking, and soon other dogs joined in and started in his direction growling menacingly. By the time the mullah was on level ground, he was surrounded by three dogs that appeared about to attack. The mullah pulled on the bridle and gazed at the dogs as benevolently as he could. From the shepherds' shelter a man emerged who raised a stick in the air and shouted "Hah!" The dogs stopped growling and followed the mullah as he rode towards the man. There were four shepherds in the shelter having lunch. They got up and greeted the mullah and made gestures of invitation for the mullah to join them in their repast. The mullah thanked them and asked, "Where is Hajji Ildrum?"

The men nodded towards the encampment across from the meadow. Mullah surveyed the area and then gazed at the sheep which were lying on the ground in their tangled mass. He noted their fat rumps, their soft, clean fleece, and full tummies which moved gently up and down as the animals breathed. Walking through the flock, he felt the gaze of a thousand pairs of live, wholesome eyes staring placidly out of wooly faces at his back.

"Where is my flock?" the mullah asked the man who was accompanying him.

"Hajji Ildrum has put them in Hamza's charge," the man informed him.

"Where is Hamza?'

"At the upper camp."

"Any losses?"

"Thank goodness no," said the man with satisfaction. "They are all healthy and fat."

"God be praised!" said the mullah. Then he added, "You don't need to trouble yourself. I'll find my way."

"God speed," said the shepherd and stopped in his tracks. As the mullah rode away from him, he watched his lanky figure swaying in the saddle. It seemed as if the mullah's shoulders got narrower as he rode in the distance until he looked like a rod jutting straight out of the horse's back.

When the mullah arrived near the tents, the people who were scattered in the area stopped and looked at him. A large dog appeared from behind a rock and came forward barking half-heartedly. The people who were standing around shifted in their places and the mullah saw Hajji Ildrum leaving a tent. The man

The Cannon

immediately noticed the mullah and shouted, "Hey, Mullah, hey Mullah Hashem!"

"Greetings to you, Hajji," shouted the mullah over the heads of the crowd.

Hajji Ildrum rushed forward and grabbed the reins of the mullah's horse. "Greetings, and most welcome, Your Grace," he said effusively.

The mullah slowly got off the horse, took off his saddle bag, and handed the bridle to Hajji who in turn gave it to a young boy in attendance. He then led mullah by the hand inside a tent made of white wool and hitched with new, clean ropes. Inside, bedrolls had been stacked around the tent and in the middle of the floor a colorful variety of food was placed on a sheet of cloth.

"You're just in time," said Ildrum. "We haven't even touched the food yet. I hope you haven't had lunch."

"No, I haven't," replied the mullah.

"Would you care for some water?"

"No, there was a spring just before I got to the camp."

In a renewed burst of enthusiasm, Ildrum said to the mullah, "Very, very welcome. Real pleasure to see you. We've been missing you a lot. The kids see you so rarely they dream about you. As God is my witness, just last night we were talking about you."

"You're very gracious," returned the mullah. "God bless you."

"I couldn't imagine I'd see you any time soon," said Ildrum.

As he was dunking some bread in his soup, the mullah said, "It is fate. It pulls you this way and that willy-nilly."

"Talk about fate," interrupted Ildrum. "It is always a factor. As long as Hajjikhujalus, Ghujabeglus, and such other bastards are around, fate is going to be around, too. Like a coin with tails on both sides, fate makes a loser out of you every time."

In an effort to soothe him, the mullah said, "We've had worse days than this and we've pulled through." Then, as if he had enough of this subject, he asked, "Have you heard the news of the general?"

"Yes, I have," replied Ildrum. "He is supposedly here to help Rahim Khan to rout us."

"But it doesn't look like Rahim Khan has accepted the offer," intimated the mullah.

"Not accept it?" Blurted Ildrum compulsively. "He's in cahoots with the government. How could he not accept it? He's accepted everything. Isn't that so?"

"No," emphasized the mullah. "He has not accepted the offer and he says since when has he been in need of someone to watch over him."

"That son of a bitch," fulminated Ildrum, "will finally accept it."

"Well," said the mullah, "whether he will or not, the crux of the matter is that the general is still here. He is sitting in ambush at Salavat, with his cannon at the ready, waiting to massacre a bunch of tribal folks who will sooner or later pass through there."

"That's a lie," said Ildrum defiantly.

The mullah, somewhat miffed by the assertion, shouted, "What do you mean a lie? A whole bunch of people have seen him with their own eyes."

Sonorously, Ildrum posed the question, "How does the general know we go through there?"

"I don't know about these things. All I know is that the situation calls for caution," said the mullah.

The Cannon

"What do you mean caution? God has not grown these arms in a man's shoulder for nothing," Ildrum said with undisguised bravado. "With my few men and rifles I'll blast my way past the general and no fear."

The mullah, his mouth full of bread soaked in soup, mumbled, "This is recklessness, Hajji."

"I have no choice. What else can I do?"

"Well, I have given the matter considerable thought," remarked the mullah. "My conclusion is that you should go by the mountain ridge and get yourself to Aji Ishma. What I mean is that you should make a detour. There is no other way."

"What if I run out of water and lose the animals?"

"With the aid of God the Merciful, nothing will happen, Hajji. You and I have the cunning of the wolves of the wilderness. If you don't want to suffer losses, you must take my advice."

"No, Mullah Hashem," said the man with emphasis. "With all due respect to your holy lineage, I will not do this. Don't you know that Havar Khan's Hajjikhujalu gang will be in Aji Ishma in a day or two. I'm just not in the mood to get tangled up with them."

Heatedly, the mullah pleaded with Ildrum. "I give you my word of honor, I swear on the head of my Holy Ancestor, that I will head for Havar Khan's camp this very day. They know me well. I have served them and have buried their dead for years. Anyway, they heed my word. With God's help I'll get them to change their route or at least delay their departure until you have passed through safely."

"Mullah, don't for one moment think that I have any fear of Havar Khan's people," bragged Ildrum. "Even if all the Hajjik-hujalus gang up on me, with God on my side, they can't put a chink in my armor. If they have 50 stolen rifles, I have a pure and courageous heart. I am bound to the Eighth Imam who will aid and protect me."

"Why are you telling me all this?" asked the mullah. "If it is for my benefit, I am well aware of it."

A few moments passed in silence while both men were deep in thought. Eventually, Hajji Ildrum broke the silence. "What do you say I should do," he asked.

"By the Holiness of God," said the mullah, "your interest is in taking my advice. After all, I am a descendant of the Holy Prophet."

Ildrum, staring into the bowl of soup, which by now was cold and unappetizing, said in a tone of resignation, "Very well."

"When are you going to get under way?" asked the mullah with concealed satisfaction.

"Tomorrow morning."

"You're going to take the whole clan, aren't you?" asked the mullah with some uncertainty.

"Of course," snapped the chieftain, "the clan, wives, children, animals, everything, obviously."

"How about … the few …. I mean my flock … which Hamza is tending …?" stammered the mullah with some embarrassment.

"I'll take them, too. Don't worry about them."

"May Imam Ali give you succor."

The two men lapsed into a pensive mood for some moments but Ildrum snapped out of it and said: "I must tell them to start packing right away."

As the chieftain left the tent, the mullah felt a sense of achievement and with a feeling of renewed vigor lifted his eyes to the sky and whispered, "Thank You."

The Cannon

All of a sudden, a goat stuck its winsome head through a slit in the side of the tent and stared at the mullah. The mullah leaned over and caught the animal by it horns. As he glared into the surprised animal's eyes he said in a mild tone, "With the will of God, I will not let even one of you go to waste."

And he kissed the goat on the forehead before letting it go.

SIX

A week later, they all came out of the caverns. The news was that Rahim Khan's riflemen had bypassed the village and Tulachi was no longer in danger. First, the men came out and congregated in the village square to assess the situation. After they assured themselves that the danger had passed, they brought out their families and belongings. Finally the animals were returned to their fold. Tulachi came alive once more and got back into its daily bustle. Children scampered about in the alleys and women, with brooms in hand, started putting an air of normalcy in the life of the village. Soon, the dust could be seen rising from houses and smoke from bread ovens. Villagers were tired but happy, as if they had returned from a long trip and were eager to settle to the comforts of home.

As soon as the tea house was set up, men started gathering there around the alderman and some village elders who had already positioned themselves on a dais at the back of the room. The alderman, fingering a rosary, said, "Thank God it passed amenably."

There was a chorus of agreement. Then he added, "God took pity on our wives and children. In the name of Imam Hussein, I beg God for an end to our predicament."

"Now, wait and see how the tribesmen will pay penance," said an elder. "Mark my word, not one of them will be exempt from God's wrath which will strike them unawares."

A second elder said vociferously, "In the name of the Holy Five*, may God exterminate them all!"

---

* In the Shiite tradition the "Holy Five" is a reference to the Prophet and his daughter, Fatima Zahra, her husband, Ali, and two of their children, Hassan and Hossein. In Shi'ite tradition, Ali, Hassan, and Hossein, respectively, are the first, second, and third successors to Mohammad.

The Cannon

"Not all are scoundrels," objected the owner of the house. "Not one person has ever been hurt by the Khalifalus. Isn't that true, Alderman?"

"Damn them all, good and bad," blurted the alderman. "May the Muslims be rid of them."

"Aren't the tribes Muslim too, Alderman?" asked the host.

"A Muslim does not strike fear in the hearts of wives and children," explained the alderman. "A Muslim does not plunder, burn, and massacre young and old indiscriminately."

The second elder gave a big yawn and said, "May God lead them to the right path."

The alderman added, "Now that they are at one another's throat, no one knows what's going to be the end."

Suddenly, there was the sound of gun fire and the men rushed outside. Up on the ridge of the hill opposite there were horsemen in fur hats holding rifles at the ready glaring at the newly resettled Tulachi. The alderman shouted, "Hey! Here they come!" As the villagers started running for cover, the assailants streamed down the hill, firing their guns.

SEVEN

Behind the green hills of Bozun, the soiled and tattered tents of the Hajjikhujalus were pitched on flat land. Some distance from the camp men were practicing shooting. The chief, Havar Khan, seated on a rock with some blunderbusses at his feet, was rapidly reloading the guns and handed them one by one to the young men who stood in a line behind him. Each man, upon getting the gun, would straddle a horse and gallop to the foot of the hill where he would fire at a target. The shot would ring out in the open space and with the smell of gun powder, the horse would calm down. The rider would then trot back to where the chief was and turn over the horse and weapon to the next man. Havar Khan repeated the exercise every other day to keep his men in shape.

At the end of the day, it was Havar Khan's turn. He loaded the gun and waited for the last man to dismount. After that he nimbly jumped on the bare back of the horse and galloped toward the far end of the field. Half-way down the track he caught sight of a rider moving in the direction of the camp. He immediately brought the horse to a halt and yelled at his men who had also noticed the stranger. "Someone's headed for the camp," he shouted in alarm.

"He's also carrying something with him," noted a young man with a short gun on his shoulder."

Havar Khan ahead and others behind him hastened toward the figure on horseback. As he galloped in the direction of the camp, Havar Khan brought the gun to his shoulder, thinking who the rider could be. But soon one of the men shouted, "It's Mullah Mir Hashem!"

The Cannon

Havar Khan slowed down as he approached the mullah who, slouching with exhaustion in the saddle, carried a black banner on his shoulder. The outline of a hand cut in brass which was fixed to the tip of banner pole reflected the late afternoon sun. As Havar Khan was getting off his horse, the mullah greeted him with weak voice. "Greetings, greetings," said the chief with genuine enthusiasm. "Welcome, Mullah. Where are you coming from? Where are you going? This is not the right time of the year for your visit."

Then the two men greeted each other and the mullah said, "These are the worst of times. One minute you're here and the next, well, no one knows."

"You're right," agreed Havar Khan. "We ourselves are going to get under way tomorrow."

"Under way to where?" the mullah wanted to know.

"Before dawn we trek to the next camp."

The other men who by now had caught up with them, greeted the mullah respectfully. Havar Khan turned the horses over to them and headed for his tent. Amid the shabbiness of other tents, his looked bright like a clump of fresh-blown cotton wool. The mullah made himself comfortable against some cushions at the top of the tent and the chief sat on the floor facing him.

"Khan," the mullah addressed the chief quizzically, "why do you want to move now? There is plenty of grass in this valley."

"There is another reason," said the chief, ominously.

"What other reason?"

"I am going to intercept Hajji Ildrum on his trek and teach him a lesson or two about the ways of this world."

"What on earth has he done?"

"What the devil did he mean by insinuating to Ghujabeglus that we are hand in glove with the Constitutionalists from

Ardebil? As a result, Rahim Khan has sent us a nasty warning message. First I'll clear my account with him before taking care of other things."

With an air of impartiality, the mullah said, "Ildrum is not on good terms with Rahim Khan. How could he have done that?"

"One of his couriers who was interrogated by Rahim Khan has told him that. And a week ago they rustled some of our sheep from the upper camp."

"Suppose everything you say is right," said the mullah in a serious tone. "But you should note what I am about to tell you. Send word right now not to pack the tents."

"Why not?" said the chief, his curiosity piqued.

"Because it is not in your interest to move out of here," said the mullah. "The Cossack general is around here with a cannon and has orders to decimate the tribal folks. You may run into him."

"I've heard the news," said Havar Khan disdainfully, "but I'm not scared. Suppose we run into him. We'll stand our ground."

"Absolutely not!" said the mullah with as much emphasis as he could muster. "Don't think I am disinterested in the matter; as you know I have few heads of sheep with you. If you act compulsively, that will be our mutual ruination, I swear to the Holy Prophet."

"So your advice is not to move out of here?" said the chief, softening.

"Exactly, Chief," uttered the mullah.

"Till when? How long should we wait?" asked Havar Khan.

"Give it a fortnight till things simmer down. I'll give you word."

The Cannon

Havar Khan turned around and called to the manservant waiting at the entrance to the tent: "Hey, boy. Go tell them not to unhitch the tents. We're staying put for the time being."

The mullah took a deep breath and felt surprisingly refreshed and rejuvenated. Havar Khan, with brow knitted, said to the mullah, "Go ahead and freshen up," as he nodded toward a wash basin in the corner of the tent.

By now, the night had fallen.

EIGHT

Three tall hills.

Three tall copper-hued hills with sharp, pointy peaks across from Tavoos Goli, the middle one taller than the other two. All with smooth, rocky sides. They commanded a full view of the vast plain of Tavoos Goli—the Ghujabeglus' summer campsite—stretching all the way to the base of Mount Sabalan which stood over the surrounding plateau like a giant with its head in the clouds. The foothills of the mountain were furrowed with small valleys through which flowed narrow streams, each one reflecting a different color. Further down, neat little villages, which in the distance looked like dark blue clumps, dappled the plain.

On these three hills, however, nothing grew and there was the ever-present smell of sulfur and copper, like a blacksmith's furnace. Up on the cliffs, there were rows and rows of potholes eroded in the rock without the aid of the human hand, always brimming with cool, clear water, that served the eagles and many nameless birds as watering holes. Even if a train of camels could get up there and drink them dry, the benevolent nature of the hills would somehow replenish the supply of fresh water that reflected the enchanting blue of the sky. When the wind blew over the puddles from a certain direction, they gave a ringing sound, as of a gentle rap on the rim of the brass bowl carried by the tribal sooth-sayer.

On a massive cliff close to the peak of the middle hill and surrounded by potholes of all shapes and sizes, stood a small tent made of white felt with a colorful rug hanging in its entrance. This was the sleeping quarter of Rahim Khan, the Ghujabeglu

The Cannon

chieftain. He spent his nights in this tent in the company of none but his two rifles.

The copper-toned cliffs of these hills became magically slippery at night to the extent that no man's footwear nor any horse's hoofs could grip any purchase on them to climb. Thus, Rahim Khan felt immune from any danger as he slept in his tent. Usually, he had dinner down in the camp before climbing up to his tent at dusk. From his perch high up on the hill he could hear every sound, the rumbling of clouds that crawled from behind the Sabalan and rushed toward the parched meadows in the plain, the din of shepherds who drove the well-fed herds back to the fold, the crackling of firewood here and there slowly burning out. He could also spot everything below him: the gleaming of a rifle barrel in the moonlight or the light reflected from the glaciers of the Sabalan, the spark of a flint stone, the turning of a poacher's eyes as he sat in ambush waiting for prey.

This way, Rahim Khan kept watch over his camp and, like an eagle, controlled his territory.

In the light of the moon, eagles gathered around potholes to drink. When midnight came, it was as if the earth had breathed and the vein of the Sabalan had begun to pulsate. Then the eagles would soar and give their place to finches that bathed their soft feathers in the water and carried the news of approaching dawn to the depths of the valleys. Soon the sun would budge from behind the mountain ridge and Uzun, Rahim Khan's personal attendant, would appear lumbering up the hill, carrying a jug of milk and a bundle of bread and cheese. He would call "Hey, hey," from behind the curtain, to which Rahim Khan would respond sleepily and emerge from the tent.

But on that day, when Uzun came up the cliff, Rahim Khan was already up and was washing his feet in one of the potholes. Uzun greeted him as he deposited his breakfast near the tent.

"What's going on?" asked the chief.

Thinking that the chief, in his usual manner, was making small talk about the position of the sun in the eastern sky, Uzun said, "Not all up yet."

"I'm not talking about the sun," said Rahim Khan. "I'm talking about the folks."

"They have been up since midnight," Uzun informed him.

"What do you mean they've been up?" asked Rahim Khan wiping his nose, he continued, "What have they been doing all night?"

"They've been up waiting for you, Chief."

With some irritation, Rahim Khan said, "So what? Why didn't they stay in bed? Sitting and waiting for me doesn't accomplish anything."

"Didn't you tell them to wait," countered Uzun, "and not do anything until you arrived?"

"At least they could have brought the cannon out," said Rahim Khan.

"They did," said Uzun. "It is sitting by the creek. They have oil and rags ready for you to start."

Placated, Rahim Khan said, "hand me the milk jug."

After he splashed some water on his face, Rahim Khan took a few gulps from the jug and then asked Uzun, "Is it up now?" this time referring to the sun. Uzun turned to look at the mountain ridge and replied, "Just about."

Rahim Khan took his toes out of the water and dried them with a felt cloth. Uzun knelt in front of him and began to massage his master's feet.

The Cannon

"Do you know what I intend to do?" Asked Rahim Khan.

It was the chief's habit to confide with his valet in their morning routine. Uzun replied in a familiar tone, "No, I have no idea."

"This Russian general is here to challenge my dignity," said the chief resolutely. "I intend to make him understand that he's made a blind error. Obviously, he's never come across a tough nut to crack."

"That is a good idea, Chief. Whatever you do is just fine," said Uzun approvingly.

"They think I can't stand up to them by myself, " said Rahim Khan with a sense of outrage.

"Who thinks that?" asked Uzun.

"Those bastards, I mean," Rahim Khan barked.

Confused, Uzun asked, "What do you mean?"

"I mean, "said Rahim Khan in a rising tone, "on the one hand, they appeal to me to control these ragtag tribes so that they don't throw their lot with the Constitutionalists. On the other, they send a useless, Russian ruffian over here to help me, so to speak. I'd say to those bastards, if you don't think I am up to the task, then why don't you let me go after my own business?"

"You're right," agreed Uzun, "they should let you go after your own business."

"But you know, Uzun," continued Rahim Khan, "they have a trick up their sleeve. You follow?"

"What trick?"

"After all is said and done, they want to do away with me."

Flabbergasted, Uzun said, "Are you serious, Chief?"

"I honestly believe that," said Rahim Khan.

"Those low-down scoundrels," said Uzun vehemently.

"Now the general orders me what to do and what not to do," said Rahim Khan indignantly. "But we're not taking it sitting down. Do you know what I did? What message I sent the general?"

As he squatted on the ground, busy wrapping cheese and bread into a sandwich the size of a cat's head for the chief, Uzun said, "No, I don't know."

"I virtually told him to turn around and get lost or he will have to reckon with me first," said the Khan defiantly.

"That's the way to go," said Uzun unreservedly. "First massacre his troops and then go after your own business."

Inspired with a sense of his own importance, the Khan bragged, "He's forgotten they call me Rahim Khan of the Ghujabeglus!"

"He's just too dumb," said Uzun, caught up in the spirit of the moment. "If he'd been smart, he would have realized that right away."

"We will now go down," said Rahim Khan with an air of authority and command, "and get the cannon serviced and readied. Now that the general has deployed a cannon, so will I. He has now met his match, blow for blow, shot for shot. He must either get back to where he came from, or face annihilation."

"I reckon it is better to annihilate him," advised Uzun.

"I swear to the severed hands of Abolfazl[*] that I will do exactly that," said Rahim Khan resolutely.

"I know Chief," said Uzun. "You always do what you promise."

Both men fell silent for a few moments. Then Rahim Khan, calmly and deliberately, asked, "What is its position now?"

---

[*] The half-brother of Imam Hossein and a martyr at Karbala.

The Cannon

Uzun glanced over the chief's head at the Sabalan and said, "Now it's way up in the sky."

The two men rose to their feet. Uzun handed the cheese sandwich to the chief and headed toward the tents to get the rifles. Rahim Khan started to descend the hill as he gnawed on the sandwich. Uzun, with the two guns slung over his shoulder, followed him. Some old eagles resting on the side of the hill, left their perch screaming, and flew in the direction of the sun.

NINE

Just before dark, the mullah arrived in Tulachi. The signs of plunder was everywhere, burned houses, collapsed roofs, blackened walls. He got off the horse and looked around in total amazement. Then, leading the horse by its reins, he proceeded to walk gingerly through the rubble in the narrow lanes and cautiously inspecting the destruction around the village. He was so overcome with apprehension that he hardly breathed.

By the time he got to the mosque in the square, he was sure the village was completely deserted. The stench of smoke was everywhere and the breeze wafted airy flakes of ash from the rooftops and scattered them everywhere.

As he stood by the mosque he wondered what had happened to Tulachi, a village noted for always being populated and prosperous, what disaster could have struck, who could have wreaked such devastation on the place. Perhaps it was the general, that infidel, his gun may have done it.

But he could see the damage was of the kind perpetrated by human hand. If it had been artillery shells, things would have looked different.

He tied the horse to the burned stub of a tree, hung a feedbag around its neck, and entered the mosque carrying his saddlebag and the banner. From a collapsed part of the roof the newly risen moon cast a beam of light that look like a large pillow on the floor. Two small animals, probably mice, were cavorting in that patch of light and making squeaky noises which to the mullah's ears sounded like peals of human laughter. They jumped up and down, biting each other's tails and making noises of pleasure. The mullah watched them until they became aware of his presence and ran scuttling under the pulpit.

The Cannon

The mullah dropped his saddle and banner in a corner, took off his turban, and squatted on the floor, staring through an opening in the wall at the surrounding ruins. Although he had not eaten anything since morning, he did not feel hungry. An insidious fear had permeated his being. Is this the work of the general? Is it possible that at this very moment he is sitting quietly in the corner of this abandoned mosque, the general is busy chasing the tribes, firing on them with his big cannon, looting and killing the sheep, his and theirs? Isn't he massacring the shepherds and mutilating the children? In his mind he heard the roar of a shrapnel so vividly that he actually jumped up and looked outside. But there was nothing outside and he sat down again. As he leaned against the wall, he felt his eyelids getting heavier and in a state between sleep and wakefulness, he could hear the sound of countless men herding thousands of sheep that came rushing into the village, bleating and tinkling the little bells around their necks.

After a few minutes, there was actually a cloud of dust that drifted past the place where the mullah was sitting, followed by a couple of tall shepherds in tribal headgear carrying leather lassos and driving a flock of well-fed sheep coated in heavy wool into the village square. One of the shepherds spotted the mullah and stopped to greet him. "God give you good fortune," the mullah returned his salutation. He then asked, "Where are you coming from?"

"From the summer camp site yonder," replied the man.

"What fat sheep," observed the mullah. "Whose are they?"

"They're all yours," said the shepherd, laughing. "Don't you recognize them?"

Surprised, the mullah ejaculated, "Mine? You mean they're all mine? So where are you taking them? Ha? Where are you taking them?"

"We're taking them to another camp," explained the shepherd. "We are moving to the lower grasslands."

"That infidel general has blocked the migration path, don't you know," asked the mullah with alarm.

"Yes, we do," answered the young man, unfazed.

"So, why are you heading that way?" the mullah asked. "He is sitting in ambush and means to blow the world apart with his gun."

"With God's grace, he can't even harm their dung," said the shepherd confidently, as he pointed to the animals. "They have all been blessed. You can see they all wear amulets."

The mullah glanced over the bustling herd and noted that it was so.

"You put them around their necks yourself," the shepherd reminded him. "This way, nothing's going to harm them. Even if the general with all his hustle and bustle lands a shrapnel right in the middle of the herd, he can't blow up a single one of their droppings!"

"But he has a big gun with him," said the mullah anxiously. "He can blow up those mountains yonder, let alone a bunch of poor animals."

Unconvinced, the shepherd said, "We're going to go through, and you'll see nothing will happen." He then swung the lasso around his head and gave a yell at which the flock broke into a run. Before the mullah could say anything else to deter them, they had rounded the hill in a cloud of dust.

Fatigued and despondent, the mullah sank to his knees. Once again, the silence was overpowering. The mullah felt something had changed, and his world was not the same any more. He noticed that the two mice had emerged from under the pulpit and resumed their play.

TEN

At first a patch of cloud appeared. Within minutes there was a thunderclap and the sky darkened. The shower that followed was heavy but brief. Soon, the sky cleared and the sun came out.

Dolmachev, bored and impatient, stepped out of his tent. The Cossack were scattered all over the camp. Near the creek Rahim Oghlu and three Cossacks were repairing the wheel of a wagon.

Dolmachev burped loudly and yelled, "Hey, Cossacks!"

Rahim Oghlu turned and when he saw Dolmachev, he ran toward him. The ground was wet and his feet sank in the mud, making it difficult to pick up speed. He stopped at attention near Dolmachev. He was holding a piece of metal in his greasy hand.

"Hey boy, what news?" asked Dolmachev.

"We still haven't found a scout, sir," replied the Cossack.

"Why not?" barked Dolmachev.

"For four days, sir, three of my men have been scouring four or five villages around here for one and have returned empty-handed," said Rahim Oghlu, looking visibly mortified. "In the first and second villages they all ran into their houses and wouldn't come out despite all the shouting and yelling from the Cossacks. In the third village they were so scared they couldn't even talk. In another village they all pretended as if they didn't know a thing. In the last village they thought the Cossacks were tribesmen on a rampage. So they stoned them out.

"Now, what are we to do?" Dolmachev yelled with anger.

"You see, sir," said the Cossack, placatingly, "this pass is on the tribal migration path. If we wait, they'll show up sooner or later."

"I have been waiting for ten days now," said the general irritably, "and nothing's happened."

Lost for ideas, Rahim Oghlu suggested, "Perhaps they are late. Also, perhaps they have been tipped off and have taken a detour."

This idea infuriated the general. "It's all 'perhaps this, perhaps that,' Rahim Oghlu," he shouted. "I have come here to carry out a mission. I am not here to run a god-damned holiday camp for a bunch of thick-necked Cossacks!"

"Exactly, sir," said Rahim Oghlu, avoiding his superior's angry gaze.

After the outburst, the general spoke ominously and with deliberate calmness: "In two days, I am going to make a move."

"In which direction, sir?" asked Rahim Oghlu, who was eager to change the subject.

"I'm going to look for the Ghujabeglus' pasture. I want to see this Rahim Khan who is so full of himself."

"But he has refused to work with us."

"Not only that, he's also ordered me to pack off and go back to where I came from," said Dolmachev, feigning meekness.

"What are you going to do to him, sir?" asked the adjutant gleefully.

"I just want to show him what it means to deal with a general," replied Dolmachev with a sinister smile.

"Shall I start packing up the camp?" asked Rahim Oghlu.

"Not today," said Dolmachev. "Wait till dusk tomorrow."

Then, Dolmachev whistled for his dogs and, leaving Rahim Oghlu behind, started walking up the hill as the dogs crowded around him.

At the top of the hill, the large cannon was firmly in place. The gunner and gun crew were removing the cover they had

The Cannon

spread over it for protection from the rain. After the cloud burst, the sun shone brightly and looked like a projectile just fired from the gun, soaring in the direction of infinity.

ELEVEN

It was past midnight, but Mullah Hashem had a long way to go to Salim Aghaji. The moon, on its way down behind the hills, gave off a glow with a red tinge. The air was redolent with the aroma of dew in the grass and a babbling stream ran nearby. Against the faint glimmer of the horizon, a few trees moved side to side gently despite the lack of any wind, as if a myriad of invisible crawling night creatures had climbed their branches to watch the setting moon. The mullah, pulling the horse behind him, was looking for a rock as a hitch and a grassy patch where he could nap till sunrise. At the foot of a hill he noticed a bulk that seemed suitable for his purpose. As he approached it, a voice called to him, "Hey, Hey."

"Oh, my God! Who could this be?" the mullah thought, as he stood riveted with fear.

"What are you after this time of night, Mullah?" the voice asked. It came from a dark figure with only the whites of the eyes visible in the faint moonlight.

"Who are you?" asked the mullah

"I am from the wilderness, from the pastures," said the dark figure.

"Which tribe are you from?"

"I don't belong to any of them; I belong to Kamalan. He's my master; he's my father."

"Kamalan? Who is Kamalan?"

"He's everything. He's from the wilderness too."

"Where's his homestead?"

"He's everywhere," said the dark figure. "He's behind this hill listening to us, up on that tree waiting for the moon to set and

The Cannon

the sun to rise. He's on top of a hill, slaughtering an old sheep, smoking a water pipe in Salim Aghaji's teahouse.

It took the mullah some moments to recover from the surprise and disorientation resulting from the encounter. But a vague fear immobilized him; he could neither retreat nor stand his ground. Cautiously, he addressed the figure: "How far is it to Salim Aghaji?"

"If you leave now, you'll be there tomorrow noon," replied the figure, and as if he could read the mullah's thoughts, he continued, "Make no haste. Stay with me tonight. Kamalan will be here in an hour to talk to you."

Obediently, the mullah sat on a rock facing the man. In the dim light, the mullah could make out a gaunt figure who had a long thin face with a full beard and large bulging eyes, marked with dementia.

"Why are you going to Salim Aghaji?" asked the man.

"Nothing …. I was just going there …." stammered the mullah.

"Has someone died?"

"No, not as far as I know."

"But I know for sure no one has died. So, don't hurry," commanded the man. Mesmerized, the mullah echoed, "Thank God no one has died."

"By the way, Mullah Hashem," said the man, "What have you been running after all these years? I have been keeping up with you. Kamalan has kept up with you. You have been running around for some time. I know you covet something. What is it that you covet?"

"I covet nothing," said the mullah, agitated.

"Yes, you do," said the gaunt man accusingly. "You know it, and Kamalan knows it, too."

"What does Kamalan know?" said the mullah, hoping to change the subject.

"Kamalan knows the more worldly goods one owns, the more anxiety one has," said the man with an air of authority. "He says that one should not try to make an exception of oneself when general disaster is impending. Kamalan says it is futile to worry one's head too much."

"Kamalan is right," the mullah agreed, in an attempt to placate his companion.

"In a way," said the man, "Kamalan is like you. Like you, he follows the tribes in their migrations and collects the fleece of the lambs which catch on the underbrush. He has a liking for those soft fibers and weaves them into a blanket for himself, which he carries with him. Kamalan says, 'I have a big, comfortable blanket, but no lambs or sheep. The mullah has many sheep, but no blanket. Kamalan says the mullah roams the wilderness and trembles with the cold."

Then the man fell silent. It occurred to the mullah that his efforts were not futile; he was trying to save the sheep from Dolmachev's plunder so that Kamalan would not be left without a blanket.

"Kamalan is hungry now," said the man, disrupting the mullah's train of thought. "Do you have something for him to eat?"

From his saddle bag the mullah produced some bread and cheese and offered it to him.

"We will wait a while until the moon has set. Kamalan does not eat in the moonlight. He prefers to eat his bread and cheese in darkness."

TWELVE

After the tents were set up, the men of the Alarlu tribe gathered around their chieftain, Hajji Ildrum, who was staring thoughtfully in the direction of the setting sun. One of the shepherds brought him a water-pipe. Hajji rested his rifle on his lap, took the pipe and fingered the hot coals on top of it. He then took a deep draft and blew out the smoke. Addressing the men around him, Hajji said ruefully, "That Descendant of the Prophet! He has got us into a fix, hasn't he? We have no reason to fear the Cossacks. If we had taken our normal course, we would have been where we want to be by now."

"Perhaps this is in our interest in the long run," said one of the elders who was sitting on the chief's right side. "It is true that we have had considerable difficulty in finding good grassland and are short of water, but perhaps this is still a better situation for us."

"I'm thinking what we should do if we run into Havar Khan's Hajjikhujalus when we get to Aji Ishma," said the chief.

"Send out a scout to get us some news," said another one of the elders.

A young tribesman, who was sprawled on the ground and was poking a blister on his foot with a twig, said in a cavalier tone, "Suppose we run into them, we are every bit their match."

"For the time being, I don't want any conflict with other tribes," said Hajji Ildrum.

"If we had gone through Salavat Pass," said the first elder, "we were sure to face the general, and that would have had the same result."

"If we find ourselves in a pickle with the general," said Ildrum, offering the pipe to the elder, "we can always backtrack or make a run for it. But if we run into Havar Khan's men, we have to engage them and fight to the bitter end. We can't afford to risk our reputation with the tribes if we hedge, can we?"

"We can make some kind of compromise with Havar Khan," said the second elder. "We really don't have bad blood between us."

"No way!" said Ildrum emphatically. "He's taken it for granted that we are in cahoots with Rahim Khan. He doesn't know that we thirst for each other's blood. He thinks it is our fault that the Ghujabeglus are on the war path with him. It is none of my business. That pimp Rahim Khan is on a war path with all the world."

A flock of birds, with long flowing plumes on their heads, flew overhead and headed towards the distant hills now speckled with gold dust in the waning sunlight.

The elder with the water pipe turned to Ildrum and asked, "What if Havar Khan is not in Aji Ishma when we get there? Are we going to camp down?"

"God bless," exploded the chief. "What are you talking about? We must hurry through and head for the homeland."

Suddenly, they all fell silent and listened for the faint footfalls of a horse approaching from behind a nearby sand dune. From inside the camp some dogs set up a fierce howl. The men stood up and gazed in the direction of the sound. Soon, a strange mullah on a white horse appeared on the ridge. A bird with flowing plumes circled around his head screaming.

THIRTEEN

The men surrounded the mullah near the brook and stood in expectant silence. The mullah, who by now had removed his turban and taken off his cape, shouted in a resonant voice, "God be praised!"

An old man with a dark bundle under his arm beckoned to a young man who, in turn, gave a nod to three men standing at a distance around an aged camel with an old shoe suspended around its neck. The men slowly led the camel toward the congregation and one of them that held the reins made it sit on the ground. There was a battered casket strapped on the camel's back with two small banners flying at its sides. The men untied the casket, placed it on the sand near the brook, and removed its lid. Inside, was the corpse of an old man with a long beard and callused forehead dressed in a shepherd's clothing. His lips had turned inward and white foam had dried around his mouth. It looked as if he had transpired while sucking on something. The mullah again shouted, "God be praised," and was echoed by the others. He then got to his knees and started undressing the deceased. There were several leather whips around the waist which the mullah removed. Turning to the crowd, he asked, "Did this blessed man have a son?"

A young man, with large green eyes, stepped forward. The mullah, handing him the whips, announced, "This is your patrimony." He then spread a piece of cloth over the corpse's loins and proceeded to remove the trousers. Afterwards, he filled a copper bowl from the brook and sprinkled it over the body. The crowd chanted, "Praised Be Mohammad and All of His Divine Kin." The mullah leaned over and picked up a pebble from the bed of the stream. With it, he rubbed the face and feet of the dead man as he sonorously sang out the chant. As the men joined him in the incantation, the mullah rolled up the cuffs of his trousers and stepped in the water, gently shifting the body to the middle of the stream. The water backed up against the man's shoulders before running over him. "Thank God, thank God," said the mullah jubilantly, "this blessed man is already saved. Look how he smiles in the water!"

The men craned to look at him. The clear water in its course had formed tiny whirlpools over his heavily lined face and wrinkled lips, giving an impression of a vague smile, as if he was happy to find something to sip on. Then the mullah gestured to some men who stepped in the water and helped him lift the body onto the sandy bank. The old man with the dark bundle produced a shroud made of linen and handed it to the mullah. Somberly, the mullah wrapped the body in the shroud and knotted its top and bottom. "May God bless him," said one of the men, "how soon his business was taken care of!"

"He was as light as a child," noted the mullah, as he stepped aside and sat by the stream. The old man turned to him and said, "Nobody expected to see you here for the rest of this year."

"This year is very different from the others," he observed. "in the name of Mohammad may God take pity on us Muslims because the situation is very confused."

With a dejected tone, the old man said, "I am afraid we may not live to see the winter camp, Mullah. Our wives and children will be scattered all over the place."

"Any news of Dolmachev?" said the mullah, changing the subject.

"Well," said the old man, "as the rumor has it, he is going to have it out with Rahim Khan. People are scrambling to get out of the way."

"Who says he's going to have it out with Rahim Khan?" asked the mullah in alarm.

The Cannon

"I don't know, exactly," said the old man, "but the news is everywhere that Ghujabeglus are getting ready to face the general. Rahim Khan has again brought out his banged-up cannon and no one knows what's going to happen."

The mullah jumped to his feet. "Are you sure?" he asked with apprehension.

"Well," replied the old man, "this is what I hear. Hard to tell how much of it is true."

By now the corpse had been placed back in the casket. The camel was ruminating calmly and unconcernedly, with the dead man's shoe dangling from its neck. Suddenly, the mullah turned to the old man and said, "I must hurry, then. I may be able to do something."

"Aren't you officiating at the burial?" asked the man, surprised.

"No, I'm running late," replied the mullah.

The young man with green eyes said, "We were hoping for a sermon at the memorial service."

"I have to check on the farmers," the mullah told him as he made himself comfortable astride the horse. The old man handed him the turban and cape which he had neatly folded. The mullah dug the stirrups in the sides of rested and energetic horse. Soon he had crossed the highlands and was descending toward the Moghanlus' encampment. He slowed down for a moment, racked with indecision. Some dogs came running toward him, barking. Eventually, he decided to go in and give a recitation of the laments. Perhaps an appeal to the Lord of the Martyrs would help solve some problems. But then what? He had lost sight of his original intention and did not know why he was running hither and thither. Was he looking for the Ghujabeglus or Dolmachev? Who was he trying to save? The tribes? Himself? His sheep?

By the time he had collected his thoughts, he was in front of a large tent decorated with patches of black felt and banners flying all around the outside of it. Inside was full of women who had knotted their long tresses together, howling and beating their breasts as they turned round and round in circles. The mullah pulled up at the entrance of the tent, took off his turban, and, without getting off the horse, began the recitation: "Woe for the thirsty lips of Hussein …."

The sound of whimpering and crying women was the only thing audible for miles around.

FOURTEEN

Darkness had engulfed the deserted fort of Barzad. An eerie silence reigned. A large buzzard, almost the size of a sheep, was perched on a broken wall holding the unidentifiable remains of an animal in its claws. From the cellar of the ruins came a mysterious rumbling, as if a monstrous chain was rattling under a rapid current of water. In the far horizon a faint copper-hued aurora diluted the darkness and shone like the glow of dying embers, still hoping for a renewed blaze.

All of a sudden, the silence was broken and from the cover of darkness emerged a band of riders carrying rifles on their backs. They galloped past the fort and headed west.

The buzzard lifted the carcass and hastened to the impenetrable darkness of a basement in the innards of the fort.

FIFTEEN

After he rounded the bend in the road, he saw the gun, that towering, fearsome mass. It looked as if one hill had mounted on another. He stopped the horse and stood watching it in amazement. This was the first sight the mullah had caught of his nemesis. Facing the sun, almost grinning, at one moment the cannon seemed to the mullah like a giant with a long neck and broad, sinewy chest who had dug his feet firmly into the ground. The next moment it seemed like an agile leopard, out of the forest and into the hills. There were a few men milling around it. In comparison, they looked like infants just starting to walk. The mullah closed his eyes and passed his hand over his face. His worst fears had been justified. How could anyone stand up to this monster? Nevertheless, he did not change his mind about going ahead with the plans he had made as he trudged through the wilderness. He prodded the horse and started his descent into the valley. He was now moving straight in the direction of the cannon. He felt as if the monstrous gun breathed and its breath shook his body and set off a tremor in the surrounding hills. He saw himself as a puny creature who has no choice but to enter the den of a sleeping lion and face the stormy rage of the animal startled out of his rest.

In this state of mind, the mullah reached the foot of the hill. For a while, he was not able to decide which way to climb. He looked around and could not see any living thing in the vicinity, except the few phantom-like figures floating around the gun. Eventually, he decided on a narrow upward path and started to move. The horse was exhausted and in its effort to climb, contorted its body to maintain balance. Half-way up the hill, the yell of a man broke the silence of the hills. Undeterred, the mullah yelled back. A dog barked once and fell silent. The mullah expected to be set upon by the Cossack dogs. So, he lifted the tails of his cape and raised his legs on the sides of the horse as he continued his progress upward. But no dogs appeared. Then he heard a strange huffing noise coming from behind. He turned and saw two Cossacks on horseback closing in on him fast. One of them shook his gun at him and asked, "Hey, where are you going?"

The mullah, pale and trembling, said, "I'm going up there."

"What are you going to do up there?" asked the second Cossack.

The mullah, pointing to the gun, said, "I'm going to see that."

"It's of no use to you," said the first Cossack, laughing. "There is nothing up there that's any of your business."

"I don't want to do anything to it," said the mullah. "I'm just going up there."

"Which village are you from?" asked the first Cossack.

"From no village," answered the mullah. "I'm from the wilderness."

"From the wilderness?" said the Cossack. "What does that mean?"

"I preach, I recite the laments of the Lord of Martyrs, I appeal to the Imams."

The first Cossack turned to the other one and said, "He's a mullah. He begs among the tribes." He then turned to the mullah and said, "You can't get up there that way. Follow me."

With the Cossacks on either side of him, the mullah started climbing down the hill. After they passed through two towering sedimentary crags, they reached the encampment area. The place was strewn with large and small tents, horses grazing unattended, and large, boisterous Cossacks. The arrival of the trio attracted the attention of the men who rushed forward and surrounded the mullah. They all had faces with prominent features, large teeth, and poor complexion. They had rolled up the cuffs of their trousers and many walked barefoot. They wore hats and stared at the mullah open-mouthed. The two Cossacks accompanying the mullah were looking around and when one of them spotted Rahim Oghlu, called out to him. The other Cossacks started calling Rahim Oghlu to get his attention.

Soon, Rahim Oghlu was shouldering his way through the throng of Cossacks toward the mullah. He had a whip in his hand and appeared irritable. "Hey, Rahim Oghlu," said the first Cossack, "we found this guy on the way to the gun emplacement and we brought him here."

Rahim Oghlu inspected the mullah top to toe and asked, "Where are you from?"

Before the mullah could say anything, the second Cossack said, "He's from nowhere. He just roams the plains."

"I hold religious services for the tribes when they are in summer camps," added the mullah.

"Which summer camps?" Rahim Oghlu asked.

"All of them," said the mullah.

"That means you know where all the camps are," Rahim Oghlu concluded.

"With the grace of the Lord of the Martyrs and the Imam of the Downtrodden, I certainly do," said the mullah with some condescension.

Rahim Oghlu thought for a moment before turning and jostling his way through the crowd toward the large, white tent dominating the camp.

The mullah turned to one of the Cossacks and asked, "whose tents is that?"

"The general's," replied the Cossack, "General Dolmachev's."

The Cannon

One of the Cossacks nearby, who was scratching his neck, remarked, "How the hell does he know what 'general' means? Tell him something he understands."

"He asked a question; I gave him an answer," shot back the Cossack on horseback. "I don't care if he understands or not."

"Hey, hey," yelled Rahim Oghlu from where he was standing near the white tent, and motioned the mullah to approach. As the mullah and the two Cossacks started toward the tent, the other Cossacks dispersed.

"Get off," ordered Rahim Oghlu. The mullah dismounted, taking his saddle bag and banner with him. Inside the tent, Dolmachev was lounging on a divan, flanked by two black dogs with metal collars. All three gazed intently at the mullah as he entered. The mullah muttered something by way of greeting which Dolmachev ignored. Instead, he asked, "Hey, Seyyed*, do you know all of this area?"

"Not everywhere," said the mullah, "just the summer and winter camps."

"Are you a tribesman yourself?" Dolmachev wanted to know.

"No, I am not," the mullah informed him officiously. "I am a singer of the praise of Imam Ali, and a descendant of the Prophet."

Dolmachev, dismissing the mullah's self-promoting announcement, asked, "Do you visit the Ghujabeglus and Hajjikhujalus and Alarlus?"

"I visit everyone," said the mullah, "all Muslims."

"What do they pay you?" asked Dolmachev.

"I'm not a mendicant," replied the mullah indignantly. "I take what I am given, but never ask. I go from place to place. The Prophet's descendant never begs."

---

* A Seyyed is a descendant of Mohammad, a term of honor.

Dolmachev, unimpressed by the mullah's protestation, got up and looked him over as he would a sheep and observed, "You're so thin! These pimps don't take care of their beggars. I'll tell Rahim Oghlu to feed you so you get some flesh on those bones."

"May God reward you," said the mullah meekly.

"I'll give you money. How do you feel about money?" asked Dolmachev jocularly.

"I appreciate all the blessings of God," said the mullah.

"You stay with us," said Dolmachev, temptingly. "Take us to the tribes, show them to us, and we will give you money and food so you'll become rich and plump."

"But they are not always in the grasslands," said the mullah. "They're like lizards. They slither from place to place, hard to catch."

"Then how do you find them yourself?" asked Dolmachev suspiciously.

"I just roam the plains until I find them," explained the mullah.

"Without pastures their sheep will not survive," went on Dolmachev, still unsatisfied.

"Right now," explained the mullah, "there is great contention among them. They try to avoid one another."

"In whatever way possible," said Dolmachev, vaguely threatening, "you must lead us to them. This region is full of hills and valleys. Can't go very far without a scout."

The mullah, feeling more secure, asked, "Which one do you want first?"

"The Ghujabeglus," replied Dolmachev without hesitation.

"I must go look for them and come back with the news," said the mullah.

The Cannon

"The sooner the better," barked Dolmachev. He then shook his head and started pacing for some moments before slumping into the divan. The dogs licked his boots and cuddled up to him.

"Hey, Cossack," said Dolmachev, as he turned to Rahim Oghlu. "Take this beggar and feed him. Then bring him back to me."

Rahim Oghlu and the mullah came out and walked through the camp in the direction of the tents that housed the kitchen. At the opening of one of the tents they stopped and Rahim Oghlu addressed a fat man inside who was leaning over a huge cauldron: "Hey, Sha'ban, feed this fellow well. General's orders."

The man turned and looked at the mullah. "Sit right there," he told him.

The mullah squatted outside the tent and placed his bag and banner next to him. The man brought a pot full of nondescript mush and put it in front of the mullah.

SIXTEEN

The men came hastily and scrambled in front of Havar Khan's tent. Alerted by the noise, Havar Khan poked his head out and shouted, "What's the matter? What's happening?"

The man in front of the gathering said, "Abolfazl is back." Havar Khan quickly surveyed the group and spotted him, disheveled and covered in dust, standing at the back of the crowd.

"Hey, Abolfazl, didn't you go to Aji Ishma?" asked Havar Khan as he emerged from the tent.

Abolfazl pushed his way through the crowd toward Havar Khan. "I've just come back," he replied.

"What was going on there?" asked the Khan.

"Tell him what you saw," urged one of the men.

"The Alarlus had been there," Abolfazl reported.

"What?" said the Khan with disbelief. "The Alarlus had been there?"

"Yes, I swear," insisted the young man. "I saw with my own eyes four of their wagons which were packed up and ready to go. The others had already gone."

"What about Ildrum himself?" asked the Khan. "Didn't you see him?"

"He'd already gone to Aghbulagh."

"How did you know?"

"I heard."

"How did they get to Aji Ishma?"

"I don't know. Perhaps by adetour."

"Did you see them clearly? Are you sure you were not mistaken?'

The Cannon

The young man, somewhat hurt, repeated emphatically, "I did not head back until I had made sure."

The chief squatted on the ground and others did the same. With a loud voice he said, "A pipe."

A short man sitting next to him jumped to his feet and headed for one of the tents.

"How has Ildrum dared to go to Aji Ishma?" said Havar Khan asked of no one in particular.

Abolfazl said, "He has grazed Aji Ishma bare. Not a blade of grass was left."

Addressing the crowd, Havar Khan asked, "Don't you think Ildrum has other plans?"

There was no answer.

"I reckon he plans to pull a fast one. But I swear to the honor of Ali, I will rub his nose in the dirt so hard he'll never think of doing it again," said Havar Khan, his words ringing in the ominous silence of his men. He then turned to an elderly man nearby and asked, "How many days since Mullah Mir Hashem was here?"

After counting on his fingers, the old man said, "About ten days."

"If it hadn't been for his insistence," said Havar Khan, "I would have never stayed here."

With an appeasing tone, the old man said, "But that is in the past, Khan. You'd better exercise patience and restraint now."

At this point, the man who had gone for the pipe returned and placed it in front of Havar Khan. After a few deep drafts, Havar Khan turned to Abolfazl and asked, "So you said Ildrum had gone to one of the nearby villages?"

"Yes, to Aghbulagh, they said," replied the young man.

"Looks like Mullah Mir Hashem is in on this with Ildrum," said the Khan thoughtfully.

"No way," said the old man vehemently. "He has broken bread with you and is beholden to you. Besides, he is a descendant of the Prophet and incapable of such unmanly behavior."

"He's got us scared of the general's gun," Havar Khan went on, unimpressed with the old man's argument. "Then how come Ildrum has gotten past him unscathed?"

The old man, still trying to defuse the situation, said, "As Abolfazl reported, Ildrum has taken a detour."

Havar Khan let go of the pipe and got to his feet. "We will pack up the camp," he said, "and send a forward patrol to look for a safe passage. Pray that I don't come to grips with Ildrum, or else I will make him forget who he is."

Taking their cue from the chief, the men got up and scattered through the camp whooping and yelling loudly.

SEVENTEEN

The door was shut and the water had been diverted. The mill house, silent and deserted, looked forlorn and smaller in dimension than its former size.

The walls had lost the white, powdery look of a flour mill and the surrounding chestnuts looked different in their orange hue of early fall.

The mullah got off his horse and looked around. A deadening silence prevailed. He walked to the mill house door and pushed it open. There was no sign of life inside. The windows on the opposite wall had been bricked up. In the darkness he could only see a shattered water jug and a tattered skull cap. Even the rats had deserted the place. The ceiling was sagging ominously, waiting for the slightest blow to cave in. What had happened? What had become of Baba? Such questions swirled in the mullah's head. Since on his way into the village he had noticed groups of women and children walking to or from work, he had concluded things were normal in Tak Dam. So, he reasoned, something must be wrong with Baba. He got back on the horse and headed for the village by a narrow path that circled the stream and the orchards. On the way, he exchanged greeting with a few more women and children. In the middle of the square four or five men had slaughtered a cow and were busy skinning it. Some women, accompanied by their children who looked underfed and scrawny, were expectantly waiting around the spectacle each holding a bowl. They became increasingly jittery as more and more of the flesh of the animal was exposed. They jumped up and down and pushed one another around as they made strange, howling sounds.

As the mullah approached, the men stopped their work to greet him. They all had rolled up their sleeves and were holding blood-stained knives in their hands.

"May God increase His blessings to you," said the mullah, as he dismounted.

Pointing to the carcass, one of the men said, "Your Grace, this cow was about to perish when we got to it."

A second man, showing the mullah his knife said, "Not us but this." The other men chuckled.

The head of the cow had been severed and was lying on a rock with swarms of flies and wasps around its eyes and hanging tongue.

"Well, Mullah," said the first man, "you are in this area again."

"I was heading up toward Movil," said the mullah. "I thought I'd stop by and see how you all are."

"May God keep you," said the second man. "Don't you want to stay with us a few days?"

"No, I must hurry through," said the mullah. "Incidentally," he went on, "I checked on Baba's mill and it was closed. I hope there's nothing wrong with him."

"Oh," interrupted a third man, "so you haven't heard what trouble Baba's been in."

"Something else has happened to him," blurted out the mullah, genuinely concerned, as he took a few steps toward the men. The children stepped away from him and gathered around the rock where the cow's head had been placed.

"This is how the story goes," began the first man. "A few days ago, Baba gets it into his head that he should visit Hazan again. He gets underway and this time, as fate would have it, he runs into Rahim Khan's men who somehow discover that he had been taken to see Dolmachev. The poor man is hauled in front

The Cannon

of one of the khans who has the shit beaten out of Baba, thinking that he works for the Cossacks. After he is satisfied that is not the case, and that Baba works in this village, lets him go."

"Where is he now?" asked the mullah.

"He is at home," said the third man as he wiped his knife on the tail of his frock. The first man pointed to a corner of the square where Baba's dwelling was. The mullah's glance moved to the little house, then to the men and the dead cow, and back to the house again. "I'd better go see him," he said. He then turned his horse over to one of the children and walked in the direction of the house. He passed through the broken fence and entered the front yard where he coughed several times to announce his presence. Two old women in black scarves looked out of a window.

"Sister," said the mullah, "I want to see Baba."

The women disappeared from the window wordlessly. The mullah coughed several more times and went up a staircase in front of the house to a door that the old women had opened for him. He stepped into a room in the middle of which Baba was lying on a blanket face up with his arms stretched out like two sticks of dry wood. He was staring at the ceiling through half-closed lids and his large, henna-stained feet were propped up on a stack of bare mud bricks. "No one must know that I have been to see the general," the mullah thought to himself as he bent over to look at Baba. "Otherwise, they'll have my hide before I have a chance to explain."

EIGHTEEN

In Aghbulagh there was a sudden burst of commotion. First it was only a hubbub outside the village. But soon the frightful shouts and cries of peasant women and children could be heard as they rushed to take refuge inside their cottages followed by men running for cover. Then Havar Khan's horsemen entered the village from several directions, galloping through the narrow lanes toward the central square where they were joined by Havar Khan himself, brandishing his rifle. He was wearing a large hat and his sleeves were rolled up. He waved his henna-stained hand in the air as he glanced around the square several times. "Where is the alderman's house?" he shouted.

"We haven't seen anybody," said Abolfazl.

At the top of his voice, Havar Khan called, "Alderman! Hey, Alderman!"

From behind a cottage, the alderman emerged with arms akimbo in a gesture of servility, visibly trembling with fear. Havar Khan drove his horse in his direction and, as he dismounted, hollered at him, "Where the hell is Hajji Ildrum?"

"Hajji Ildrum is not here, Khan," whimpered the man.

"He is here," yelled the khan. "I know he is. It is in your interest to tell me where he is hiding out."

"I swear to God he is not here," insisted the alderman.

"Do you mean to say he's not shown up here these past few days?" asked the khan incredulously.

"I swear," said the alderman in a plaintiff tone. "I have no reason to lie to you."

"Hasn't he even been in the vicinity?" the khan asked, still furious.

The Cannon

"We haven't heard anything, Khan. Nothing at all," replied the alderman.

"Hey, Abolfazl," the khan shouted as he turned his head. Abolfazl took a step forward. "Where did you say Ildrum had gone?" asked the khan, rhetorically. "Aghbulagh," replied Abolfazl. The khan turned to the alderman and asked, pointedly, "What is the name of this place?" With a voice hoarse with tension, the alderman replied, "Aghbulagh."

"You see, you old dog?" yelled the Khan, as if presenting incontrovertible evidence. "I'll have you skinned right now. I'll turn your children into orphans."

With his horse whip Havar Khan struck the alderman in the face. The old man sank soundlessly to the ground, covering his face with his hands. The khan ordered his men to dismount and search the dwellings.

"Khan," pleaded the alderman, "have pity on our women-folk and children. We are the decedents of the Prophet; we are helpless; we are Muslims. Don't displease God, Khan. We are innocent. Have pity. Be fair."

Havar Khan took a length rope from the back of his saddle, looped one end of it around the man's neck, and tied the other end to a hitching post nearby. "I have no pity. I know no fairness. I am the cruelest of them all," he muttered under his breath as he handled the rope. "And now if you move from here, I'll knock your brains out. Don't you dare move!" he said emphatically.

He then beckoned to his men who left the horses in the middle of the square and rushed into the huts, kicking down the gates and doors. Simultaneously, cries of terror and agony filled the air. The alderman, looking like a beast of burden with the rope around his neck looked on, praying vehemently. Soon the noise subsided and only an occasional laughter or cursing of the tribesmen could be heard. The men were turning the huts inside out, looking for their quarry.

After a while, Havar Khan returned to the square, more enraged than before. The alderman bent down and rested his hands on his knees.

"Hey! Old man," yelled Havar Khan, "if you don't want me to turn this place upside down, tell me where he is. Or I'll burn this place to the ground and drag him out of his hole."

"Please have some consideration for us," spoke the alderman as plaintively as possible. "We have no business with the Shahsevan. We are nobody's enemy. Now that you are here, have a bite of bread and cheese with us. It does not behoove the godly to strike fear in the hearts of innocent women and children."

With indignation, Havar Khan yelled, "Do you think we are after your miserable bit of bread and cheese? Are you trying to bribe me with that?"

"Khan," said the alderman, with as much emphasis as he could muster, "I swear to God, to the Holy Prophet, to the severed hands of Abolfazl* that Ildrum is not around here. What on earth would he come here for? What is there to do in this godforsaken place?"

"You can't pull the wool over my eyes with this kind of talk, old man," retorted the Khan.

"I'm being honest and straight with you, Khan. Why don't you take my word for it?" the alderman said.

"I'm being honest and straight with you, too," snickered the Khan. "Wait and I'll show you what I mean by honest and straight." As he spoke, the Khan took the rifle off his shoulder and aimed it at the old man. The alderman, yelled reflexively, "Oh, God, the Most Merciful!"

---

* Imam Hossein's cousin and one of the martyrs of Karbala.

The Cannon

At this very moment, the blast of a great explosion shook the village. Havar Khan jumped back and the alderman sank to his knees. Almost instantaneously, Havar Khan's men rushed out of the dwellings. Havar Khan, still disoriented by the sound, shouted, "What the hell was that?"

The men looked at one another, dumbfounded. Havar Khan let out a loud yell: "Take horse! Ildrum is in the neighborhood," and pointed to the hills beyond Aghbulagh. Within seconds the entire contingent was galloping out of the village in a cloud of dust.

A moment later the villagers rushed to the alderman's side, removed the rope from his neck and stretched him out on the ground. "I am fine," said the alderman assuringly, taking a deep breath. "The damned heathen was about to kill me but the Protector of the Deer[*] came to my rescue."

---

[*] The reference is to Musa ibn-Reza, the eighth imam of the Shiites. The legend has it that once he extended sanctuary to a hounded deer.

NINETEEN

It was early evening and there was a congregation of men in the large tent that served as the community mosque. The flaps on two sides of the enclosure had been raised to allow a cross-current of air which blew in from the Tavoos Goli foothills, bringing with it the smell of early autumn nightfall. In front of the mosque a band of young men in black shirts were slapping their backs and chests with chains in the performance of a religious ritual. A group of women and children huddled together a few steps from the mosque.

A blind man, with hands that seemed too large for his tiny stature, was blowing into an old, battered bugle and made a doleful noise as of an old cow mooing in a distance. The sound of a horse galloping came from behind the mosque and presently Uzun, Rahim Khan's valet, came into view, carry a rifle over his shoulder. He interrupted the proceedings as he yelled, "The Khan is coming!"

"Hallelujah," croaked an old man, sitting by a large banner in front of the mosque. The young men in black joined the old man in the chant and sat down on the ground. Within minutes, Rahim Khan arrived on horseback, accompanied by Mullah Hashem. They dismounted as the assembly uttered a communal greeting and stood up.

Rahim Khan and the mullah passed through the crowd and entered the mosque. Rahim Khan put his rifle across his knees and turned to Uzun. "Get me a water pipe," he told him. The people filed into the mosque and sat facing the khan as Uzun rushed out after his chore.

The khan turned to the mullah and said, "Well, Mullah Hashem, tell these good people what you just told me."

The Cannon

The mullah rose to his feet slowly and took a deliberate step forward, as if buying time. The women on the outer edge of the crowd covered their faces. The men huddled closer, looking at him intently. The mullah stared at the crowd. Men and women, with open mouths and squinting eyes, stared back. He was at a loss for opening remarks and could not get his voice up. He gazed at the weather-beaten faces of the tribal folks. The old man sitting by the banner sensed the mullah's unease and shouted, "Praised be the Prophet," which the crowd echoed automatically.

The mullah cleared his throat. "I have bad news for you," he said cautiously. A broad-shouldered tribesman, sitting next to the blind bugler, yelled in the direction of the mullah, "Very kind of you, Mullah Hashem. The Khan will give you four fattened sheep right now in return for your troubles." A few people laughed tentatively at the intended sarcasm.

Without looking to see who made the comment, Rahim Khan yelled back, "Shut your mouth for a minute, Teymur." As if he had not heard the Khan's remark, Teymur asked the men around him, "What does the Khan want me to do?"

"He wants you to shut your mouth for a minute," obliged the old man sitting by the banner.

"Very well," said Teymur, "I'll shut up, but it's better for the mullah to shut up and keep his bad news to himself."

Inside the tent, the mullah stroked his beard and continued: "Dolmachev is on the move. He is heading this way and he plans to stage a raid on you."

"How do you know?" shouted Teymur from the outside.

"I heard it along the way," the mullah said.

"Was this your bad news?" asked Teymur laughingly.

"Yes," shot back the old man by the banner with irritation. "And they want to come here and cut your tongue and throw it away to give us some peace."

"That's what you think," snickered Teymur. "As long as we have the Khan, they can't do a damned thing."

"Shut up!" yelled the khan from inside.

"Yes," the mullah went on, "Dolmachev is on the move. He is going around Tikanlu to attack the Ghujabeglus. As soon as I hear this, I rushed to the Khan's presence to give him the information."

At this time, Uzun came bustling inside the tent, carrying the water pipe for the Khan. "Well, now, Mullah Hashem," said the khan, "let us rest a while." The mullah returned to the khan's side and sat next to him. Rahim Khan turned to the crowd and said, "We'll get under way tomorrow morning and stand right in the motherfucker's way to let him know who runs the world."

TWENTY

In the morning, they brought the cannon down from the hill. By the time they removed the ropes, it looked like a fatigued giant let loose in the plain. The sun had just risen and was slowly spreading on the encampment area. Some Cossacks were packing tents. The horses had been led to a nearby watering hole and a short, stocky Cossack was slapping a thick, black liquid from a large bucket on their hoofs. The men who had lowered the gun from its emplacement on the hill were sitting around smoking their pipes. The gunner was struggling with the gun carriage, trying to dislodge something from the mechanism. On an elevation right above the gunner, stood Dolmachev in full dress uniform. The golden epaulets on his tunic glowed in the sunlight like two molten blobs of gold. Rahim Oghlu stood in attention nearby. "We must get going in an hour," said the general to Rahim Oghlu. "I have a feeling the mullah has given us the slip." "Whatever you say, sir. We will be ready to go whenever you wish."

"There was a directive from General Federov yesterday recommending that we finish our business with these people here as soon as possible."

"At your command," said the adjutant, irrelevantly.

"A contingent of Mojaheds set siege to Tabriz and tried to take it. They were mostly from the tribes, I hear," said the general.

"How could they have gotten that far?" asked Rahim Oghlu.

"Federov tells me it is all instigated by a mullah in Meshkinshahr," replied Dolmachev.

"Could it be the same mullah we are looking for?" speculated Rahim Oghlu.

"No way. This mullah is a beggar. The other one has his own organization and is called Mullah Imamverdi," informed the general.

Trying to make light of the situation, Rahim Oghlu said, "His account should be settled soon."

"No problem. But first we must take care of these tribes," said Dolmachev.

Down below, the men who were smoking their pipes slowly got to their feet to help the gunner. From the far end of the encampment the strains of a Cossack song could be heard. Dolmachev turned to Rahim Oghlu and said: "Bring me a bowl of water and tell them to get my horse ready. As Rahim Oghlu sped away, Dolmachev approached the gun slowly. Together, the Cossacks had managed to remove a heavy ballast from the gun mechanism and the barrel now was parallel to the ground.

"Bring the mules," the gunner ordered the Cossacks. The men started to leave. Dolmachev addressed the gunner: "With all this huffing, puffing, and sweating you haven't got too far, have you?"

"I'll make it all up, General," answered the gunner. He then gave his loud, dry laugh.

TWENTY-ONE

Havar Khan and his men rounded the high hills of Aghbulagh and arrived at the dark entrance of a large cave which looked like a frozen skyward yawn. At Havar Khan's beckoning, the men slowed down and took positions on the brow of hill around the cave. Havar Khan turned to his lieutenants and said, "I have a feeling Ildrum is hiding in this cavern."

"How do you know?" blurted Abolfazl.

"From up there," said the khan testily, "we had a commanding view of the whole plain. There is no place else he could hide."

"But Havar Khan," Abolfazl persisted, "what would he be doing around here all by himself? Besides, how do we know the blast came from his gun?"

Havar Khan, trying to control his temper, said testily, "I have no idea what he is doing here by himself. Besides, that volley was like the thunder of a Russian field gun recently supplied to him."

"But Khan," said Abolfazl doubtfully. "It sounded like anything but a field gun."

"How do you know?" protested the Khan, "Have you ever heard the sound of a field gun?"

Abolfazl cast a glance around the circle of men. "Whatever you say," he consented. "At your command, Khan."

"Stick around the cave for a while," ordered Havar Khan. "I'm going to see if there is another opening on the other side of the hill." He then motioned to some men to follow him. Abolfazl and other men, with guns at the ready, stood at the cave entrance as the horses' footfalls receded over the ridge. Although the sun was directly overhead, the breeze still had the morning chill. Before long there was a murmur in the distance and as everyone looked towards the sound, Khan and his company of men returned and took their positions around the cave. Havar Khan turned his ear toward the opening and listened intently. He heard what sounded like the breathing of an animal and gestured to others to listen. "It's him," he whispered softly.

"What's he doing there?" wondered Abolfazl.

"Snores like a bear," said the Khan.

"What'ya gonna do, Khan?" Abolfazl demanded to know.

Without heeding him, the Khan took a deep breath, and with his head inside the cave, yelled as loudly as he could: "I-L-D-U-R-U-M!"

His voice rang inside the cave and returned: "… D-R-U-M."

"That was him?" asked Abolfazl, excited.

"Nah …. That was my echo," returned the Khan.

They waited a minute or two and the Khan, his head jutting forward, yelled louder than before, "Hey Ildrum, if you wanna live, come out now."

"… out now," came back the echo.

"You're not gonna get me off your back!" yelled Havar Khan into the cave and waited for the echo to die down before he shouted "I am not going to hurt you if you surrender."

"… render," said the echo.

"We can't get him out this way," said Abolfazl resignedly after a few moments.

"If he is in there, he is not going to be scared with these threats." Pointing to his rifle, he continued, "We'll take care of him with this."

"How?" barked the Khan, "we can't go in and he won't come out. How do you want to take care of him then." No answers were forthcoming.

The Cannon

Havar Khan once more yelled into the cave. "Hey, Ildrum" he shouted, "get out of there if you're a man. I am not gonna hurt you. I just have an account with you to settle."

"… to settle," resounded the echo from the walls of the cave.

"Impossible, by God. He won't come out this way," Abolfazl said in exasperation.

"Then I will post a couple of men here to knock him off when he eventually comes out," said the Khan.

"But nobody is sure if he is in there," Abolfazl said.

"Oh, shut up!" hissed the Khan impatiently, "I am from the desert and smell a scent like an animal. Somebody is in there." Sure enough, a rasping sound could be heard from deep inside the cave.

"There is somebody or something in any of these caves," Abolfazl said, shrugging his shoulders, "we can't search every cave and get them all out."

Havar Khan, getting increasingly annoyed, said forcefully: "But Ildrum has passed through these parts. We cannot afford to get off his tracks."

"We can do one thing," said Abolfazl thoughtfully. "Why don't I and a few chaps rush the cave? Even if he gets a chance to fire, he will hit only one of us. The rest can get him." Havar Khan said nothing. Abolfazl pointed to some men who dismounted and got their rifles off their shoulders. As if on cue, they rushed whooping wildly into the bowels of the cave. Soon the voices died down and there was an ominous silence. No shots were fired and there were no groans of injury. In a minute or two Abolfazl appeared, dragging an old woman behind him. She was thin and bent, clutching to her chest the dry roots of a plant that almost looked alike a lifeless claw. Insanely, she chuckled, with her eyes closed in the glare of the sun.

TWENTY-TWO

When the camp was dismantled and packed, a bugle sounded and the Cossacks rushed to mount their horses. Rahim Oghlu, mounted on a black horse, used his baton to order the line-up of the mounted Cossacks. After some weeks of inactivity and indolence, the men looked inert and puffy. The cannon, tied to eight mules was waiting at the rear of the column. The gunner, wearing a crimson cape, jerkily moved around the gun carriage.

The bugle sounded for a second time and the Cossacks came to attention at Rahim Oghlu's gesture. Dolmachev, in full uniform and high, riding boots came into view, astride a white horse, sitting on a saddle trimmed in silk with ornamental designs. The men held their breath as Dolmachev ambled forward and faced them. He inspected the formation in one glance and asked in a loud voice, "All presented and accounted for?"

"Yes, General," answered Rahim Oghlu.

"Anyone sick, or dead?"

"No, Sir,"

"Do these jackasses know the plan of action?"

"Yes, General, they have been advised accordingly."

"Tell them once again," ordered Dolmachev.

"By order of General Dolmachev," announced Rahim Oghlu in a loud, stilted voice, "the regiment is moving to another camp in pursuit of insurgents. Everything went well in this encampment and the general has expressed his satisfaction. In the next campaign things must go even better. The General has forbidden sickness, overeating, drinking, or horsing around. The General will not tolerate laggards and gluttons. The General says that in action every unit must obey its commander. The General

The Cannon

says the Cossack is not allowed to get killed; he has only the right to kill. The General has given the command to move."

At the sound of the bugle, Dolmachev positioned himself at the head of the column. With another blast from the bugler, the unit began to advance in a cloud of dust.

When the column reached the edge of the plain, it stopped. With his baton Rahim Oghlu pointed to a narrow footpath that snaked its way into the interior of the valley. But suddenly Dolmachev raised his arm in alarm and the column came to a halt in the shelter of mounds of earth bordering the plain. They were all gazing at a speck at the far end of the valley that soon appeared to be a lone rider.

"Is it them, Rahim Oghlu?" asked Dolmachev.

"It is only one man, Sir," said Rahim Oghlu.

"We must use caution. It could be their vanguard," speculated the general.

"Caution for what, Sir?" asked Rahim Oghlu. Ignoring him, the general barked, "The cannon, the cannon," and there was a burst of activity. Rahim Oghlu rushed to the rear of the column and exhorted the gunner to hasten in deploying the gun. Some Cossacks swung their whips in the air and directed the mules to pull the gun carriage to the narrow opening of the valley where the gunner, his cap pushed back on his head, unhooked it from the yoke and busied himself making it operational.

"Ready?" asked Dolmachev.

"Presently, General," said the gunner. Some soldiers brought heavy bags to immobilize the wheels of the gun carriage, while the rest organized themselves in two rows facing the approaching rider.

"At your command, General," proclaimed Rahim Oghlu, "Ready to fire!"

The Cossack raised their rifles and took their positions for action. Dolmachev, peering through the binoculars, suddenly yelled, "Hey! It's the mullah, the mullah. Hold your fire."

The gunner and the soldier heaved a sigh of relief and got to their feet.

TWENTY-THREE

By the time they had continued their advance along the tribal pathway, the sun had risen above the summit of Mount Chakhmagh and was approaching the middle of the sky and there were no more echoes of the horses' footfalls in the valley.

Dolmachev and the mullah were at the head of the column and the gun was being pulled at the rear. Dolmachev, pensive and frowning, asked the mullah if they were on the right track. "Yes, General," the mullah assured him.

"What is this tribal path called?" the general wanted to know. "Gharagul, Sir," said the mullah.

"And where does it lead?"

"To Tavoos Goli, General, where the Ghujabeglus' camp is."

"How long before we get there?"

"It all depends, General," answered the mullah.

A period of silence ensued. Without turning his head, Dolmachev glanced at Mullah Hashem sideways, trying to size him up. The long face covered with a graying sparse beard, narrow shoulders, and bony, wrinkled hands somehow contrasted with his beady, bright eyes, betokening considerable native intelligence. Abruptly, the general turned to him and asked with an accusatory tone: "You are Mullah Imamverdi Meshkini, aren't you?"

Jolted by the question, the mullah blurted, "Who?"

"Mullah Imamverdi?" repeated the general.

"No, General," protested the mullah, "I'm Mullah Hashem, reciter of the praise of Imam Ali and his kin. That's all."

"So, who is Imamverdi?" Asked the general with a heavy dose of suspicion.

"He is the imam and prayer leader in Khiav."

"Are the tribal areas in his territory?"

"No," said the mullah emphatically. "He does not set foot out of Khiav. He is a freeholder in the township. I am a nomad."

As if contesting the verity of the mullah's statement, Dolmachev stared him in the face and said: "But I have reliable news that he has been moving about the tribal areas and has some contacts there."

"I don't think so, General," the mullah demurred. "He is not that poor and niggardly to roam among the tribes to make a living, Sir. He could stay put the rest of his life and have enough to live on."

"But he is not working the tribes for handouts; he is recruiting fighters to dispatch to Tabriz for the Constitutionalists," mused Dolmachev. The mullah thought for a moment and replied, "But I wouldn't know anything about that."

As they started moving again, the mullah glanced furtively at Dolmachev whose frown had deepened, his eyelids puffy and drooping. He rocked with the motion of the horse, looking grim, as if displeased with the mullah's answer. To placate him, the mullah added, "General, Sir, I can't imagine Mullah Imamverdi..." But Dolmachev cut him short. "Enough. No more of that," he barked. The mullah fell silent.

In a slow canter the column moved along the trail that was covered with fine dust. As they advanced, the plain opened up before them and displayed here and there clusters of yellow wild flowers ringed with broad green leaves waving in the wind and in the bright sunlight looking like puddles of molten gold. Dolmachev, staring straight ahead, yelled, "Rahim Oghlu!" Digging the spurs in the side of the horse, Rahim Oghlu sprinted forward.

The Cannon

"Yes, Sir," he said with alacrity.

"All in order?" Asked the commander,

"All in order, Sir," the adjutant answered.

"That's all," said the general, dismissively. With that, Rahim Oghlu fell behind again.

"Hey, Mullah!" snarled the general.

"Yes, Sir," replied the mullah.

"Keep your eyes open not to lead us down the wrong trail, do you hear?" said Dolmachev menacingly.

"No, Sir," said the mullah emphatically.

"Once in the Caucasus campaign a tracker made a mistake and I had his ears cut off," Dolmachev warned.

"No, no, Sir, I won't lead you astray, Sir, I know the way. Barring any accidents, God willing, we'll get there," said the mullah.

All of a sudden, the bleating of a sheep echoed in the valley. Mullah Hashem, agitated and fraught with anxiety, stretched open his arms reflexively, as if protecting his own herds of sheep against the danger posed by his present company. Dolmachev raised his arm and blew on his whistle. The long columns stopped in its tracks.

TWENTY-FOUR

By sundown the camp had been set up and guards posted on the periphery. The chatter and occasional laughter of the soldiers filled the valley. The tents had been raised on a flat stretch of land and Dolmachev's, at the far end abutting a mound, was made distinct with a colored light hanging at its opening.

The burnt edges of scattered clouds and the smells of cooking wafting from the kitchen promised a pleasant, restful night. There was a chill in the air and the regimental dogs gave out occasional yelps, an indication that a storm was brewing. In his tent, Dolmachev had taken off his boots and was reclining on the cot under a long, heavy cowl. He would cover his toes under it with every blast of chilly air blowing in the tent. The black dog, his favorite, was crouching near him on the floor, its eyes closing every time Dolmachev's short, stubby fingers scratched its head.

Rahim Oghlu entered with a tray of food and a jug of wine. Nimbly, he set a short small table for the general. As if on cue, the dog moved away from the cot.

"Where is the mullah?" Dolmachev asked.

"He is in the mess tent with Sha'ban, the orderly, Sir."

"Make sure he doesn't get away."

"I'll watch him."

"Looks like he has something up his sleeve. Watch him very carefully yourself."

"Yes, Sir."

"How's everything?"

"Everything's in order, Sir."

"Listen to me, Rahim Oghlu," said the general deliberately. "Men are not to get drunk tonight. Remind them that they would get flogged."

Wordless, Rahim Oghlu gave a bow and backed out of the tent, heading toward the kitchen area. He passed a group of soldiers gathered around an old Cossack perched on a small stool singing and accompanying himself on a small accordion. Other men with food trays were scattered around the camp. He noticed that the mullah was sitting by himself on the ground a dozen or so yards from the kitchen with his sleeves rolled up eating his food in large mouthfuls.

"Are you taking good care of the mullah?" asked Rahim Oghlu.

Pointing to the mullah with the toss of the head, Sha'ban said, "There he is having his meal."

"But why like this?" said Rahim Oghlu with an air of dissatisfaction. "Call him over. He is a guest after all and you've got to be friendly with him. General's orders, you know."

"But that is how he wants it himself," protested Sha'ban. "He thinks of us as unclean," he said, pointing to the wine jug.

"Bring him to me, after he's finished with his dinner," ordered Rahim Oghlu as he headed for his tent.

Sha'ban filled his cup and walked over to the mullah. "Dolmachev is looking after you," he said. "You two have hit it off pretty good."

TWENTY-FIVE

In the large central square of Gharadarvish hamlet a dense crowd of people from Khiav, Pari Khanlu, and other villages and communities in the vicinity had gathered. A pulpit had been brought from the mosque to the middle of the square in anticipation of an address by Mullah Imamverdi Meshkini. He had arrived in the village the night before and was staying with the Gharadarvish alderman, Mokhtar. A blustery wind was blowing and rounding up the scattered clouds in the western horizon, causing the darkness to settle in the valley earlier than usual. A severe storm was expected by midnight. A few oil lamps, placed behind the windows of the mosque to be protected from the wind, cast a shimmering glow inside the mosque.

The crowd squatted in groups around the square and the hubbub of conversation echoed from the walls. Rumors were rife about the Mullah Imamverdi Meshkini's imminent talk. A few stars were now visible in the darkening sky. The crowd rose to its feet and gave out a shout of praise at the sight of Mullah Imamverdi and his entourage entering the square from a narrow alley. He was tall and lean, wearing a long-sleeve cowl. His long white fingers were hanging at his side, almost touching his knees. When he arrived in the middle of the square he took off his turban and cowl before he mounted the pulpit where he stood. His long white caftan reached down to the ground. "Folks," he yelled at the top of his voice, "you may sit down if you are tired. You may stand up if you are not. But do listen very carefully to what I have to say."

No one sat down. "Oh, you Muslims," roared the mullah with a voice more resounding than before. "After a few weeks of roaming the countryside, I am here the bearer of bad news. I

The Cannon

have passed through villages and townships burnt and destroyed by enemy fire. I have walked among starving tribal folks unable to sleep at night for fear of attacks. In some areas around Alireza Abad and Khoruslu famine has already set in. Some strange diseases and maladies are now decimating the people of Unar and Khud Unar. From Tabriz and Ardebil* Russian generals have been ordered to slaughter farmers and force tribal nomads to settle in their communities. At this very moment General Dolmachev with powerful artillery is scouring the plains to kill all. The Shahsevans are now divided against themselves, thirsty for one another's blood. All these atrocities are being perpetrated by the Shah. May God Almighty, at the behest of the Martyr of Karbala, curse them all who have brought such misery upon the Muslim folks!"

"Amen!" roared the crowd in unison.

"Now, in Tabriz," went on the mullah, "some have taken up arms to clean up this pestilence of aggression and infidelity, drive out the godless generals from the Shiite homeland, and exterminate the enemies of the nation and faith. Day and night, weapons in hand, they are fighting, short on supplies, short on provisions, short on munitions, but long on their faith in God and the blessings of the Holy Imams and the Rightful Saints. It is now up to all of us to join the holy jihad and do the best we can for our Muslim brothers. If one or two people come forward from every community to help the Mojahedin, we could eradicate the tyranny and infidelity and vindicate the rights of Muslims. In the past ten or twenty days a number of the Shahsevan have joined the movement. It is now up to you to show support for the cause. I am leaving tomorrow to carry the

---

* Two major cities in the Azerbaijan Province under the control of the Russian expeditionary force supporting the central government during the Constitutional Revolution.

good news to other towns. Now let those who want to join the ranks of Muslim fighters step forward!"

Mullah Imamverdi paused as the crowd, stunned and hesitant, fidgeted in place. "Listen to me, people," he resumed. "Jihad is the pillar of faith, as is prayer, as is fasting, contingent upon every Muslim. He who dies on the path of righteousness, dies pristine and sinless and the Prophet of Islam will be his advocate before God on Judgment Day."

A short man with broad shoulders, his face indistinct in the gathering darkness, stood up. "Hey Mullah," he shouted. "What do you want us to do empty-handed?"

"We'll give you arms and ammunition," the mullah assured him.

"How do we feed ourselves?" he asked. "We're not all that well off."

"You will be fed and provisioned," returned the mullah.

"What about our wives and children? What are they to do?"

"Those with families will receive assistance," stressed the mullah.

"I'm ready to join," said the man, as he pushed his way through the crowd.

"May God's grace be with you," said the mullah encouragingly.

"I'm not doing this for God's grace," said the man as he approached the pulpit. "I don't know which side's up in this world, who tells the truth, who tells lies. I'm just down and out and hungry. So are my wife and child. That's why I am here."

Not fazed by the comment, the mullah added, "And in the process, you deserve yourself afterlife rewards."

"Forget afterlife rewards, mullah," said the short man. "Right now, I could do with some bread and cheese."

The mullah turned to the crowd and asked, "Do I have a second? Do I have a third?" With a sweeping glance he scanned the

The Cannon

square. A few hands went up from various parts of the crowd and some men started moving in the direction of the pulpit.

TWENTY-SIX

Tired and hungry, Kamalan is lying at the foot of Uzun Gulakh Hill. He is staring at the moon with heavy-lidded eyes, much like a wolf lying in ambush for a prey.

A sharp wind, dragging occasional patches of clouds this way and that across the sky, whizzes in the branches of the wild olive tree, now bare in late autumn, and heads for the plain through a narrow pass at the end of the valley.

Wrapped in a blanket, Kamalan cannot take his eyes off the moon, which has drenched him in its light. A sudden change in wind direction drives some clouds over the moon, plunging the scenery in darkness. Kamalan heaves a sigh of relief and stands up—in time to see a band of horsemen with rifles on their backs riding through the hills toward the pass. They are headed by Mullah Imamverdi Meshkini, with his turban unfurled streaming behind him as he rides. They gallop past a clump of short trees and are swallowed up by the darkness at the end of the valley.

TWENTY-SEVEN

Tikanlu Valley is long and curvy, strewn with boulders of all sizes. Small streams, some from geothermal springs, flow from foothills. The valley is overgrown with thorn bushes, some brandishing faintly colored buds in their upper branches. Almost every boulder is surrounded by clumps of wild flowers swaying in the gentle breeze blowing through the valley carrying dandelion seedpods haphazardly. There are several ranges of hillocks plunging into the plain, forming several narrow vales. A contingent of men on horseback come galloping over the ridge of a hill. They all appear wary of their surroundings and ride past boulders with such caution as if expecting assailants hiding behind each, except the forward rider, Uzun, who looks unconcerned and exudes a triumphant air, with his rifle resting before him on the saddle. Closely following him is Rahim Khan, flanked by some men. He has pulled his headgear to the middle of his brow, looking menacingly grim.

Bringing up the rear is a field gun pulled by two mules. Since the Ghojabeyglus have no trained gunner, Rahim Kahn himself operates the small artillery piece when needed. As always, Uzun serves as his gunner's mate.

The men are all armed with rifles, their legs wrapped in puttee and carrying canteens at their belts. Each has a bandolier straddling the saddle. As they canter through the valley their footfalls echo from hill to hill. They have now been riding for a few days and are within reach of the Tikanlu settlement.

At sunset they arrive at a level piece of land at the foot of a hill. Rahim Khan gives the order for encampment. The men dismount and stamp their feet to shake off fatigue. The horses are let loose and men gather, their tension dissipating with Teymur's bellowing laughter.

"What are you laughing at?" Rahim Khan asks Teymur.

"At myself," answers he.

"What for?"

"For being such a chump that believes everything."

"Such as what, for example?"

"For example Mullah Imamverdi's talk."

"Which talk?"

"What he told everyone in front of the mosque."

"Well?"

"Well, well," responded Teymur impudently.

"Don't be an ass. What are you trying to say?" said Rahim Khan, irritated.

"This is what I am trying to say: How many days have we been riding? Slowly, cautiously, scared to be ambushed. So? Where is the general? Where are the Cossacks? The big cannon?" Teymur said, with an air of disappointment.

"Maybe they have taken another route," Rahim Khan offered.

"But according to the mullah they are coming to get us this way," said Teymur.

"Well?"

"But we have seen no sign of them so far."

"Are you suggesting there's something fishy?'

"Accusing a descendant of the Prophet? Why, never!" said Teymur, almost tongue-in-cheek. "But we've seen no sign of them. I am itching for some action, Khan."

Rahim Khan pauses, deep in thought. He then turns to Uzun and asks, "By the way, after we left, what happened to Mullah Hashem?"

The Cannon

"He took off, too," is the answer.

"Where to?"

"I believe for Upper Summer Camp area."

"That is where he said he was going or did you see him go there?"

At this point Uzun cuts in: "I heard him say he wanted to check something out in that area."

"But Khan," Teymur interjects. "He did not head in that direction. He left the same way he came."

"Which trail?" asks the Khan

"Gharagul trail," says Teymur.

"How do you know?" Rahim Khan queries.

"I was with him, Khan. He stopped to check on his herd and left some orders. Then we said goodbye at the turn-off for Gharagul. I saw him go that way."

"Why didn't you tell me?" asks Rahim Khan with some alarm.

"I didn't know I was supposed to," Teymur says. "I remember it now that the subject has come up."

"Do you think he has something up his sleeve?" Rahim Khan asks. No one speaks. "Is he lying?" Rahim Khan persists.

"Why should he lie?" inquires an older man, sitting on the ground hugging his knees.

"You never know why people lie. They do it for their own reasons," Rahim Khan opines, with a sarcastic chuckle.

"But Mullah Hashem wouldn't lie," adds the old man. "He is beholden to us. I can't imagine a descendant of the Prophet to lie. What motive is there for him to lie?"

"Besides," Uzun chimes in. "the mullah might have heard about the general's plans from someone else. It might not be his fault if it is not true." Teymur mutters his agreement. "But who could have told him about it?" Rahim Khan persists.

The men speculate in uncertainty, guessing possible sources— one of Ildrum's men, a stray Cossack, "or even the general himself," Teymur ventured. Rahim Khan was not satisfied. "What the hell does Mullah Hashem have to do with any of these, or the general?"

"God only knows," Teymur said in exasperation. This precipitates a towering rage in the Khan. His face is drained of color and his eyes recede into their sockets. "If there is any trickery in this," he hissed, as he dug his heels into the earth, "I'll tear the heart not only out of the mullah but also the Holy Prophet, his ancestor!"

The men, somewhat in awe, sit in prolonged silence. The sun is now setting and the blue of the sky is deepening. The surrounding hills take on a shade of grey and the horizon turns crimson. The evening breeze picks up and whistles as it sails through the valley floor scrub. The booming call of an owl is heard from a direction hard to determine. The Khan seems calmer after the outburst, easing the tension among the men.

"Khan, it's getting dark," Uzun says cautiously, cognizant of the Khan's mood. "Shall we get started?"

"No hurry," the Khan responds calmly. "We will make it to Tikanlu by midnight." Then, addressing the whole contingent, Rahim Khan yells: "I want somebody to take off right now for Gharagul to find out the whereabouts of the General's outfit and make it back by tomorrow noon. Do I have a volunteer?"

Several men jump to their feet. Rahim Khan beckons to a young man. He has a scowling face, looking grim in the gathering dusk.

TWENTY-EIGHT

The narrow trail that connected Ziveh and Limlu passed by a large growth of heather, sedge, and other shrubs laden with multi-colored berries and covered in dark, olive-green leaves. The thicket was in the middle of the otherwise empty valley. The heavy, vibrantly live foliage hid from view numerous swamps and mud puddles that had been formed by ground seepage and rainwater. It also provided a habitat for a variety of frogs, lizards, and harmless snakes as well as ducks and pheasants that fed on the limitless supply of seeds and berries.

That morning, as it was their wont, Mir Karim and his son, 'Azim, arrived at the thicket before sunrise and began to spread a finely woven green-colored netting over clumps of bushes. By now the sun had just risen over the ridge of the surrounding hills. The clear sky and a higher level of humidity in the air assured the father and son of a more successful catch. Standing in a shallow depression near a bush, Mir Karim produced a wooden whistle from a bag slung over his shoulder and began to blow in it softly, producing a remarkably realistic cooing call of a female quail. But at this moment several shots reverberated through the valley. Both Mir Karim and his son fell collapsed on the nearby brush in wild convulsion. There was a sudden en-masse flight of birds rising from the heath. Some birds were caught in the netting, frantically beating their wings trying to escape. Soon the echo of the shots died down and the father and son were by now motionless. An eerie quiet settled on the scene, except for the flapping of the captive birds. Within seconds two tribal horsemen pulled up by the bodies of the slain men.

"Oh, damn!" said one of them. "Look, Issa, they're not Cossacks."

"It was your fault," said the second man. "You said we should shoot them."

"How was I to know? They are wearing fur hats. I thought they were the general's men."

"What shall we do with them?" The flapping sounds of the captive birds filled the momentary silence.

"Too late now," said the other man.

"We're going to catch shit from Hajji Ildrum."

"Let's get rid of them before Hajji arrives," the first man said, as they both dismounted from their horses and hitched them to a stump nearby.

They first picked up the body of the older man and heaved it over a clump of reeds around a small swamp. They heard the thump as the body fell into the swamp and sank into it. Then they picked up the body of the young boy.

"Let's throw this one in another swamp," suggested the first man. "Why?" asked the second man. "This swamp might not hold both of them," the first man explained. But before they could drag the body on the grass, Hajji Ildrum and his men were upon them. Riding at the head of the column, Hajji came to halt within a few feet of them.

"What the hell are you doing," he yelled at the two men.

"We shot someone," sheepishly the first man confessed, "By mistake. We were going to throw him in the swamp."

"Who was he? Why did you shoot him?" asked Hajji urgently.

"We thought he was a Cossack. He had the same kind of hat," said the first man, defensively. "When we came close we found he was bird hunter."

"Hadn't I told you not to make any noise going through this valley?" asked Hajji, clearly irritated.

The Cannon

"Yes, you did," admitted the man. "But we thought if we didn't kill them they would kill us."

"So there were two of them," rasped Hajji, with anger rising in his voice. He then bent down to look at the body.

"This is just a kid. Couldn't you tell?" he yelled at the man, now positively enraged.

"No, sir, not from a distance," the man said apologetically.

"How we are going to pay penance* for this, I have no idea," said Hajji Ildrum, throwing up his hands in exasperation.

A morbid silence had now fallen on the group, except for an occasional flapping and screeching of birds caught in the net, which drew Hajji's attention. "What are we going to do with these?" he asked of no one in particular.

"We can get them for dinner," the first man said, almost jokingly. Hajji beckoned to some men to collect the birds. "We don't know which village they are from," he said, referring to the dead men. "I hope this does not end up around our neck."

"Even if it does," said one of the men by way of consolation, "The farmers can't do anything about it anyway."

"That's true," conceded Hajji. "But in this day and age the fewer enemies one has the better." He stared briefly at the rivulet of blood running down toward the bushes and then turned to the whole troop. "You are not to say a word of this to Mullah Hashem," he said emphatically.

"Khan, we are not going to run into him, are we?" said a thin man on a horse.

"In any case, hold you tongue," admonished Hajji. "If he finds out that we are responsible for killing these innocent men, he

---

* In Islamic jurisprudence a sum of money should be paid to a religious authority as penance for killing a person. The relatives of the decedent will in turn be recompensed from this fund.

may turn away from us or even put a curse upon us. He is a descendant of the Prophet and his curse is efficacious."

Hajji had barely finished his sentence when a rifle shot rang through the valley. Startled by the report, the men looked up and saw one of the two sentries on the ridge of the hill tumble off his horse. The other man galloped down the hill at breakneck speed toward them. "The Hajji Khujalu! Havar Khan! On the other side of the hill!" he whooped as he approached.

Without hesitation Hajji Ildrum ordered his men to mount: "Top of the hill!" he shouted. The contingent moved with surprising agility and regrouped behind the jutting boulders on the side of the hills. The narrow valley was suddenly deserted and quiet.

"How many of them?" Asked Hajji Ildrum, as he turned to face the sentry. "Quite a few," said the man.

"How do you know they're Hajji Khujalu?"

"Oh, I know them when I see them,' said the sentry, adding, "They also recognized us."

"You see how soon we have to pay back for what you did?" Ildrum muttered, worried and dispirited. No one said anything.

"Now, some of you take positions on those boulders making sure we don't get surrounded," he ordered.

By now the sun was up and the chirping of a bird of indeterminate species could be heard from the heath.

TWENTY-NINE

They had arrived at an odd rock formation, a sort of a roofless chamber, at the summit of the hill. The gun had been placed in an alcove with its barrel extending over the edge of a crag. Dolmachev and his adjutant Rahim Oghlu were standing on either side of the gun carriage. Below them the meadow stretched all the way to a range of hills on the opposite side of the valley. Then thousands of tribal horsemen would enter the valley, shouting votive chants. Dolmachev would ask, "Who are they?" and the mullah would answer, "Hajji Khujalu." Dolmachev would then raise his hand and sharply bring it down barking "Fire!" The cannon would roar and emit a cloud of red smoke obscuring the sight. Soon the smoke would settle and there would be no one on the valley floor. Then another multitude of men would march onto the field below, beating their backs with chains* wailing a mournful dirge. Again Dolmachev would ask who they are and the mullah would say "Ghujabeglu" and Dolmachev would order "Fire!" Rahim Oghlu would light the fuse, followed by an explosion and the decimation of the crowds below. At last a tall rider in a mask on a white horse clad in armor comes down the hill with a green banner on his shoulder, chanting the laments of Ashura.†

"Who is *this* one," asks Dolmachev of the mullah. "This is the Prophet of Islam, Holy Mohammad," the mullah answers. Dolmachev raises his hand in preparation for the order to fire. But the mullah hollers at the top of his voice, "Wait! Wait!"

The mullah sat upright in the middle of his bed drenched in a cold sweat, shaking violently. He saw Rahim Oghlu on the

---

* This is in reference to a Shiite ritual of extreme unction mourning the martyrs of Karbala.
† Hymns commemorating the martyrs of Karbala.

bedstead next to his, watching him intently. "What the hell is the matter with you?" he asked. "Nothing," said the mullah, panting. "I had a dream."

"Do you always blow like a bull when you have a dream?"

"This was a nightmare," said the mullah.

"They'd better tie you up with the horses and mules. The General thought you were a man when he sent you here," complained Rahim Oghlu, as he laid back down on his mattress. The mullah said nothing, got up and went out of the tent. The moon was directly over Dolmachev's tent, casting a soft milky light on the camp. He drank some water from the jug behind the tent and used the rest for the ablutionary rite.* He then knelt on the sandy ground raising his hand heavenward and began to sob.

---

* A ceremonial washing of hands and face prior to performing the *namaz,* a formal prayer ritual.

THIRTY

They remained in a state of alert until the next morning behind the craggy hills of Ziveh. But nothing had happened. Hajji Ildrum had dispatched a rider to the tribal camp with an order to stay put until further notice. A few young men standing watch over the ridge had reported no activity except that some villagers were combing the valley for signs of the bird hunters but had been scared off by the sight of sentries watching them from the hilltop. Just before sundown some men had cautiously crept up the side of the hill to retrieve the body of their slain comrade. The men in the contingent had spent a restless, tension-filled night, hearing imaginary voices and seeing dark, mysterious figures emerging from the corpse, roaming the valley, and disappearing in the darkness. Some had even heard duck calls from the swamp. As the sun came up, the meadowland welcomed the warmth of the sunrays in anticipation of a new day.

Hajji Ildrum, too, had spent a rough night hardly able to sleep, frequently addressing his lieutenants and interrupting their sleep. He had cursed the two advance patrol men and blamed the predicament on their senseless killing of innocent people.

"Damn them! What are we going to do now?" he had said in an outburst.

"We'll do whatever you order, Chief," said one of the men in the company.

"What is the use of giving orders," retorted Hajji, "when people don't follow them. I had given specific orders not to make any unnecessary noise."

In an effort to diffuse the tension, the corpulent man, who had taken care of the birds the day before, observed that that was in the past. "We should think of what to do next," he said.

"It is risky to move forward," said Hajji. "But I don't think we'll be followed if we backtrack to the camp."

"I agree," said one of the sentries. "They would have come after us by now."

"We can't go back the same way we came," said Hajji. "We have to make a detour through the plain."

"But Chief," objected one man. "There is no water that way. The horses will die of thirst."

The Khan looked at him disparagingly and said: "For one thing, we have no other choice; for another, it looks like rain and we won't get into trouble, God willing." He then gave the order to mount.

They turned around and made their way through the valley, cautiously following a narrow path up the side of Ziveh hills. By midday they were over the ridge, climbing down the other side.

THIRTY-ONE

It was still dark when Rahim Khan's envoy had reached the hills of Gharagul. He was advancing with extreme caution, rifle in hand at the ready. He breathed so quietly as if he was passing within feet of the enemy encampment. He had spent a harrowing night on horseback. Every time the horse's hoof slipped on a rock and cause a spark, he winced as the crackling sound reverberated through the valley. He would bite his lower lip in fear and self-recrimination.

He was at the foothills of Gharagul by first light. The hills, as if arranged by human hand, stretched in a straight line all the way to the vicinity of Tavoos Goli. At the crest of almost every hill there was a dilapidated, abandoned watchtower each with its gaping entrance, looking like a hungry monster awaiting a prey.

The young man had passed by these hills every year during the tribal migration season and knew the name of all the towers. The ground circling the towers was dotted with several graves and each tower was connected to the next by an underground passageway.

The sun had not yet risen and the air was imbued with a strange coolness as the young man picked his way slowly along the hills. The main migratory path of the tribes was on the other side of the hills and he remembered how the emerald-green of the grassy track in the spring getting trampled underfoot would turn to rich amber by late autumn as the tribe returned to winter in Tavoos Goli. The early morning breeze was refreshing and it brought with it what sounded like water gurgling out of many invisible springs. He felt a chill down his spine.

It was now light and he could hear the cooing of birds from inside the ruins. Suddenly he was transfixed as he heard the whinnying of horses at a distance on the other side of the hills. His mare raised her head, pricking her ears. He thought for a few moments before starting a slow, deliberate climb up the hill toward the tower. He dismounted by the wall and hitched the horse to a boulder. He crossed the gate into the interior of the edifice where darkness still lingered and he could hear the rustling of the bats in the crevices of broken walls. He passed under a collapsed roof and entered a dark corridor. The floor plan was more or less the same in all these buildings. He had heard from the tribal elders that the corridors were used to store weapons and munitions in the tower. He negotiated a sharp turn and arrived at the opening to a large, roofless hall. From this location he could hear the footfalls of perhaps hundreds of horses moving in regular cadence in the direction of his position. He crossed to the far end of the open space and climbed a crumbling buttress to look over the wall.

The faint light of the new day had brightened the horizon and reflected strangely off the wings of a few hawks circling overhead, giving the appearance as if they were flying on two jets of pale flames rather than wings. Carefully, he bent down and, peeping over the edge of the wall, saw the Cossacks in a long column twisting and turning their way, not unlike a slithering centipede, along the hillside track.

The young man ducked behind the wall and waited for the contingent to get closer so he could get a better look. He looked up again when the column was now filing past his hideout. He saw the general, with broad shoulders and a bulging belly, riding at the head of the column side-by-side with a figure that at a distance and in relative darkness looked like a mullah wrapped in his cloak on a thin, malnourished nag. Finally, bringing up the rear was the big cannon drawn by a team of mules. He jumped to his feet, knowing that he had valuable information to

The Cannon

deliver to Rahim Khan. He had seen with his own eyes the general and his men crossing Gharagul on their way to Tavoos Goli. This would really infuriate Rahim Khan. He felt self-satisfied for delivering the kind of news that would shake him up.

He now had a full view of the Cossacks in boots, stripes, and large fur hats, with their rifles strapped to their backs. As he surveyed the column, he saw the general speaking to the mullah. Who was this mullah? He looked vaguely like Mullah Mir Hashem, what with the way he rode the horse and the small black pendant he carried on his shoulder. No, it couldn't be, he decided.

He hesitated a few moments before jumping to his feet and retracing his steps back to where the horse was hitched. Before mounting, however, he noticed the animal keenly listening to the noise of the moving column on the other side of the hill. He then jumped on the back of the horse, heading downhill.

The sun had now risen and had imbued the valley with the brightness of a youthful smile as the tribesman circled the bottom of the hill heading in the direction of the next one with the remnants of a watchtower on its brow. There, he dismounted and entered a covered passageway leading to the far side of the building where he found a mound of dirt to give him cover. Now that he was well ahead of Cossacks, he had time to position himself to observe the advancing column. He would be so close that he could clearly see the details of every face. But as the column approached, he immediately realized that the cleric was indeed Mullah Hashem with his lanky figure wrapped in his customary dust-covered cloak. The shock of recognition made him leap up without fear of detection and head for his horse on the other side of the building.

Faridoun Farrokh

The sun had now cleared the crest of the hills and had forced the morning mist to lay at the bottom of the valley like pale blue smoke. Oblivious to all this, the young man set his horse at a gallop homeward.

THIRTY-TWO

At night the men assembled in Havar Khan's tent. They squatted around the tent in a circle in the gloomy light of some oil lamps in the middle of the floor. An occasional lightning would for an instant brighten the scene, followed by the roar of thunder sending a shudder through the hills and the valley. The felt roof of the tent muffled the drumming of the torrential rain.

Havar Khan, looking visibly upset and out of sorts, sat next to a brazier of burning charcoals puffing impatiently at his water pipe resting on his knee. Every once in a while one of the men would rise to refresh the supply of tobacco and hot coals in the Khan's pipe. For three days, plagued by an unseasonable rain, they had been stranded in the environs of Limlu, unable to move forward.

"What do you think we should do now?" asked the Khan of no one in particular. "Until the rain stops," said Abolfazl, sitting near the entrance facing the Khan, "we can't do much."

"Suppose the rain stops," mused the Khan. "What then?"

"We'll then move on," ventured the man sitting next to the Khan.

"But which way?" barked the Khan. "We can't turn toward the hills of Ziveh. We're going to be ambushed there. We can't backtrack toward the summer camp. And we don't know where we'll end up if we go straight."

"Khan," Said Abolfazl, trying to be helpful. "In my opinion it is best if we skirt Limlu altogether and head for Salavat Pass. We don't have a choice. And I am not sure if the general is not waiting for us there."

"I agree," said the Khan. "This is the only option with this bad weather. If it turns to snow, we'll lose half of our herd."

"It'll be sunny tomorrow, for sure," Abolfazl opined, mustering as much optimism as possible, "and everything will be fine."

"God damn that Mullah Seyyed Hashem!" said Havar Khan venomously, drawing deeply on the waterpipe. "He really messed us up in a big way."

There was a powerful burst of lightning overhead and rain fell harder than ever, threatening the tribal tents with flash flooding from hills nearby.

THIRTY-THREE

It took the Alarlu tribe two full days to skirt Ziveh and reach Sheytan Darreh,* which was a deep, sunless ravine with a steeply rising rock face on either flank. There were blackberry bushes and similar vegetation everywhere. The dried fruit on their withered, leafless limbs made them look as if they had been sprinkled with ink. There seemed to be a spring welling from under every rock only to sink in the soft earth after a few yards. Hajji Ildrum and his contingent were already exhausted by the time they entered the gorge. Hajji himself was especially edgy and brusque, losing his temper at the slightest excuse. He seemed paranoid, turning around with alarm at every sound. He held his rifle at the ready, leading the way at the head of the column. Pointedly, he avoided the sight of Issa, the advance patrol who had escaped death earlier.

They camped inside the valley for the night. The air was cool and damp. The wind, blowing hard across the ridges of the surrounding hills, whistled overhead. They drove the livestock to an opening farther below. The sound of the bustling flocks and their herders settling the animals down for the night traveled up the valley muffled and indistinct. A sense of impending danger and anxiety permeated the camp. Past midnight, the valley took on a different mood. A faint light appeared to glow from the numerous rivulets flowing from the springs; some small rodents with disproportionately large heads climbing out of the ground, scampering up and down the camp area; then the tinkling of a bell around the neck of a mule, and a sound from the other side of the hills as of a monster snoring. Soon, the impenetrable darkness gave way to first light of day which, rather than

---

* Literally, "Satan's Valley."

descending from the hilltops to the inner crevices of the gorge, suddenly drenched the whole valley in sunlight. Not long after, the Alarlus were packed up and on their way, heading in the direction of a widening plain extending to the horizon, pathless and untraversed.

An elder tribesman, riding alongside Hajji Ildrum Khan, cautiously broke the silence. "Where are we heading for, Khan?" he asked.

"Straight ahead," replied Hajji Ildrum curtly.

"Where's that going to take us?"

"We'll see."

"All these years," said the elder, trying not to provoke the Khan, "I don't remember straying off the migratory path. Now we don't know where we're going to end up."

"End up?" shot back the Khan, "I know where. We'll end up in Gharaghurulokh."

"To do what?"

"We aren't staying there," the Khan hissed. "We're simply going to pass through on the way to Surulugh."

"But Khan, they say Gharaghurulokh is a godforsaken stretch," warned the elder. "There is not a drop of water nor a blade of grass there."

"Don't worry," said Hajji Ildrum, making light of the elder's concern. "Nothing will happen."

"I'm not concerned about myself," said the elder. "I am worried about the livestock."

They let the conversation die. What could be heard was the footfall of horses accompanied by the panting of the jostling sheep as they moved farther and farther away from Sheytan Darreh pushing into the Gharaghurulokh high-plain desert. By early evening they had arrived at a range of sand dunes seeming

The Cannon

to extend to the horizon. Hajji Ildrum gave the order to camp for the night. The light was failing rapidly. A few cloud patches in the darkening sky still caught the rays of the setting sun and looked like faint moons overhead. The desert wind sounded harsh and menacing as it stirred up the dust beyond the sand dunes. Much to their surprise, they found a small spring where they watered the horses and the livestock and refilled their goatskins and jugs.

They passed the night uneventfully but restlessly and were packed and ready by first light to start their trek deeper into Gharaghurulokh. They could only see stretches of sand and lifeless tundra specked by occasional clumps of thorn inhabited by colonies of large grasshoppers, darting in all direction at the approach of the column.

The air grew increasingly warm and the sun more scorching as it climbed to the middle of the sky. The tribe nevertheless continued hurriedly and in ominous silence.

"Khan, how many more hours before we're through this infernal desert?" the old man riding with Hajji Ildrum felt the urge to ask. "Another half a day, I suppose," replied Hajji nonchalantly.

"But look ahead, Khan," protested the elder. "This seems to stretch to infinity."

"How do you know?" retorted Hajji angrily. "You can't see anything ahead," said the elder, "no trees, no vegetation, no sign of life."

"Never mind!" said Hajji Ildrum, hoping to end the conversation. However, the old man was insistent. "But Khan," he said. "I'm afraid we might get bogged down in the middle of nowhere. I am not thinking of our people. They're hardy and can probably pull through. I'm thinking of the livestock. If we lose the herds, we're done for."

"But if we'd gone the other way, we could have all been wiped out," said Hajji impetuously. "Then what good the livestock would have been to us any way?"

This put an end to the conversation. Once more the silence was filled with the sounds of the moving tribe, which in the open, unobstructed desert landscape had no echo.

By now the sun was past the midday point and shining at their back as they pressed forward. Now the ground was more solid and the horses' hooves did not sink into it. It seemed as if they had reached the center of the desert. But the wind was still hot and blowing hard, pelting their faces with gravel and other wind-born debris.

The sunset arrived fast and unexpectedly. Yet the tribe pressed on in semi-darkness. In time, the failing light and the absence of any indication that they were nearing any usable vegetation or source of water caused them to succumb to exhaustion. Soon, the camp was sound asleep in an eerie silence. Even the restless desert winds had calmed down, as if due to extreme fatigue at the end of a busy day.

At sunrise the tribe was already on the move to take advantage of the relative coolness of the morning. But the signs of fatigue showed even in the animals. The lambs did amble and the horses were unruly and reluctant to move. Every once in a while the yell of herder could be heard as he slaughtered a sheep or a goat before the animal died of starvation or thirst.[*] The dark, warm blood would spill on the hot desert sands. The carcass would then be thrown on the back of horse and carried away. By late morning six animals had to be slaughtered. The word reached Hajji Ildrum and he ordered a halt. There was still no sign of trees or elevation on the horizon. The sun, like a vicious

---

[*] In the Islamic canon an animal that dies before being slaughtered cannot be used for food.

The Cannon

and dangerous beast, clawed its way up the morning sky, as if waiting to ambush the thirsty and exhausted tribe. Hajji Ildrum and his men dismounted and gathered in a circle.

"What do you think we should do?" he addressed the men.

The tribal elder was the first to speak: "I told you, Khan, this damned stretch of desert is impassable."

"What do you suggest we do?" asked Hajji, resigned and flustered.

"I suggest we turn around and go back to where we started," said the elder resolutely.

"Go back?" burst Hajji Ildrum in disbelief.

"There is no choice," said the elder calmly. "We can't go on like this."

"But we've come a long way," said Hajji, almost pleading.

"Yet we don't know how much farther we have to go," the elder said. "The animals are dying and if we continue we stand a good chance of dying ourselves."

Hajji Ildrum took a long moment to think before nodding his agreement. Almost immediately, the men jumped on their horses and started the process of reversing the trek. Women and children on donkeys and mules, that were bringing up the rear, now led the way, followed by the herds of livestock.

Now the tribe moved at an accelerated clip. The air was stiflingly hot and the sun as merciless as ever. Some sheep strayed from the flock, unresponsive to the whistles and yells of the shepherds or the barking of the sheep dogs. Some would collapse but the shepherds would not stop to slaughter them. After two hours they stopped for a rest and were overtaken by the sun moving in the western sky, as if showing them the way to hills and pastureland lying ahead. The wind had now died down and the desert sands felt cool and refreshing. They could almost smell the grassland and water-logged terrain of the hill country, visualizing Sheytan Darreh with its deep gorge and rising hills awaiting them with open arms.

THIRTY-FOUR

The Gharagul migratory track seemed interminable to General Dolmachev and his regiment of Cossacks. This was the third day they had been slugging along the line of hills, each crowned with the crumbling ruins of watchtowers and small fortresses. Mullah Hashem, agitated and distraught, rode alongside Dolmachev. His anxiety increased as they neared Tavoos Goli, wondering what was in store for him once they arrived there. What if Rahim Khan of the Ghujabeglu tribe was waiting for them there? He had considered leading Dolmachev away from that destination to other pasturelands. But he was not sure they would not run into other tribes. His time in the company of the general had convinced him that he would surely deploy the big gun against any adversary, regardless of size and strength.

It turned chilly in the afternoon as they passed the ruins of Fort Firooz with its high mud brick walls and sentry posts which gave an echo to the noises of the advancing column. Dolmachev and his men were surveying the ruins with some admiration when they were alarmed by the neighing of a horse from the other side of the hills. They caught a glimpse of a horseman galloping away from them through an opening between the two hills.

"Rahim Oghlu," yelled Dolmachev mightily, calling for his adjutant. He appeared instantaneously before the general. "Catch him," ordered Dolmachev, pointing in the direction of the horseman. The adjutant raised his hand, pointing to three riders at the head of column. They veered off toward the hills in a gallop. Mullah Hashem, now worried to distraction, began praying. But within minutes the Cossacks returned leading the horseman before them. Dolmachev, visibly pleased with the prompt capture, moved forward, carefully examining the man who was wearing a threadbare cape and leg warmers.

"Which tribe are you from?" asked Dolmachev. "I'm no tribesman," stuttered the man, pale with fear. Dolmachev raised his horse whip and brought it down hard on the man's face. "I asked you what tribe you're from, and where are the rest of you?" Dolmachev shouted. "I swear," said the man as earnestly as he could, "I am not a tribesman. I am just a farmer from Hiru. My village is on the other side of these hills."

"If you lie," threatened Dolmachev, "I'll have you skinned alive." He then turned to the mullah, who was cowering behind Dolmachev trying to be inconspicuous. "Hey, Mullah," said the general, "where is he from?"

"Mullah?" ejaculated the man, his jaw dropping with surprise. "Mullah Hashem?" Averting his eyes from Dolmachev, the mullah said, "No, General, he is a farmer. He is not a herdsman. I know him. He's from Hiru."

Dolmachev raised the whip and hit the man twice in the face as he yelled "Go, go and get lost." The man turned around and rode off as he kept looking back, as if not believing what had just happened.

The columns started to move again. By now the sun was setting and the mullah felt increasingly depressed. Something had cracked within him, and he was sure the word of his collaboration would spread fast in the region, ruining his reputation and tarnishing his image forever.

THIRTY-FIVE

"Hey, hey, Havar Khan!" The call echoed through the narrow valley and brought out Hajjikhujalu men from their tents. It was a bright day and the ambient moisture in the air shimmered in the morning sunlight. Men looked around in alarm and bewilderment. "Hey, Havar Khan, hey," the call rang out again.

Havar Khan, rifle in hand, burst out of his tent. "Who is it?" he asked his men. "Who wants me?"

"It's from the other side of the hill," Abolfazl, the Khan's aide, responded. "They're calling for you."

Havar Khan waited momentarily and yelled back: "Hey, hey, who's calling me?" There was no response. "Whoever it is," mused Abolfazl, "is not one us. It doesn't sound familiar."

"So why are they calling me?" Havar Khan wondered. He then yelled at the top of his voice. The answer came from behind the hills, almost immediately.

"Shall we go see who it is?" asked Abolfazl. "No," said the Khan. "It could be an ambush. Set up a perimeter in case there is an attack." The men moved in a defensive formation, at the ready. There was another call, this time nearer and louder. Abolfazl cupped his hand around his mouth and yelled mightily, "Hey, hey!"

The head of a horse appeared briefly above the jagged crest of the hill. "Who are you?" shouted Abolfazl.

"Guests," came back the answer. "Who?" Havar Khan asked Abolfazl. "They say they are 'guests'," he informed the Khan.

"Tell them to come over," ordered Havar Khan. Abolfazl repeated the order.

Almost immediately, three men in tribal outfit and armed with rifles came into view as they rounded a hill. More men had emerged from the camp and were standing in a row watching the riders intently. "Khan," burst out Abolfazl in alarm. "These are Rahim Khan's men."

"That is all right," said Havar Khan, as if to reassure Abolfazl. "Let's see what they want." An expectant silence fell upon the gathering. The three riders moved closer, stopped, and made greeting gestures with their hands. They looked calm and friendly, their body language showing no hostility.

"Welcome," said Havar Khan, pointing to his tent. The men dismounted and made formal salutations.

The Khan repeated his welcome and asked where they were coming from. One of the men, standing a step ahead of other two, cleared his throat and said, "Rahim Khan has sent us with his greetings and good wishes."

"Rahim Khan?" said Havar Khan, with some surprise in his voice. "What for?"

"We have been sent," said the man solemnly, "to inform you that he wishes to set aside any dispute and animosity between our tribes." Havar Khan, trying to suppress the sarcasm in his voice, said, "What happened? You would shoot the Hajjikhujalus on sight. Now you are proposing peace?"

"It is in our interest to set aside our old differences," said the man, trying to sound friendly. Still intransigent and resentful, Havar Khan added, "You mean it is in *your* interest to forget about the past. Rahim Khan would not send peace emissaries if it were in *our* interest." "The Khan sends his compliments," said the man, trying to be diplomatic and sincere simultaneously, "and says that it is in our *mutual* interest to cooperate. General Dolmachev and his division are heading for Tavoos Goli and he is up to no good."

"The general can go where he pleases," said Havar Khan, "Tavoos Goli is no business of ours." Unfazed, the man added,

The Cannon

"Rahim Khan respectfully informs you that this is a plot cooked up by Mullah Mir Hashem."

"Mullah Mir Hashem?" blurted Havar Khan, taken aback at the mention of the mullah's name. "What plot? What do you mean cooked up by Mullah Mir Hashem?"

"The mullah is serving as the general's guide showing him the lie of the land," said the man. A second man added in confirmation, "Rahim Khan respectfully urges you to cooperate for our mutual benefit."

Havar Khan, deep in thought, lowered himself to the ground and squatted. Hastily, other men followed suit. "What is the plan?" asked the Khan of no one in particular. "Rahim Khan respectfully suggests," said the second man, "that we converge on Tavoos Goli and stage a raid on the Cossacks and finish them off."

"Only your tribe and ours," asked Havar Khan, "or other tribes will join us?"

"You're the first Rahim Khan has contacted," said the first man. "He believes if you go along, others will follow."

"But you realize," said Havar Khan, "that the general has a lot of men as well as a large-caliber cannon. How can we overcome him?"

"Rahim Khan respectfully proposes that we first neutralize the gun," said the second man. "Then he is dead meat."

Havar Khan, seeming somewhat skeptical, scratched his beard. After a few moments of silence he addressed his men, "I knew from the start there was something tricky about the mullah."

"But it was hard to put your finger on," added Abolfazl. "He was good at hiding it."

Turning to the emissaries, Havar Khan announced, "Even if it is to serve my turn upon the treacherous mullah, I will come. Rahim Khan can rest assured of that."

The men circling Havar Khan rose to their feet and invited the three visitors to the tents for refreshments.

THIRTY-SIX

The Cossacks were now nearing the end of the Gharagul tribal migratory track. Exhausted and dispirited, they followed the general who led the column alongside Mullah Mir Hashem. Directly behind them was the cannon being pulled laboriously along the rough, bumpy track.

In the distance, the copper-colored hills surrounding the tribal summer camp gave off a faint glow in the afternoon sun. The column advanced to the base of the hills and started a climb. Soon the expanse of the Tavoos Goli meadowland came into view and with that the mullah's anxiety level reached a new high. He could not take his eyes off the summit of a hill in the middle of the meadowland. A patch of cloud cast a dark shadow on the hill. The mullah could almost feel Rahim Khan's penetrating eyes watching him from the top of that hill. He turned to the general's aide, Rahim Oghlu. "Hey, mister, can you see anything over there?" he asked.

"Over where?" inquired Rahim Oghlu. The mullah pointed the hill. Rahim Oghlu raised a pair of large binoculars to his eyes and scanned the area slowly.

"There is nothing up there. Just a cloud patch casting some shadows. They look like men lying face down," Rahim Oghlu reported.

"They may be dugouts or trenches," observed the mullah. "Look carefully. Do you see any tents on the side of the hill?"

"I see nothing. Just a few birds flying around," said Rahim Oghlu, as he looked through the binoculars. They fell silent as they continued to their advance.

The Cossacks would reach the hills and take positions to cover the meadowland, the mullah speculated. What if Rahim Khan and his force were waiting for them there? What if Tavoos Goli is deserted. How could he explain all this to the general, he wondered.

THIRTY-SEVEN

Silently and with extreme caution, four Ghujabeglu horsemen, along with Uzun, are tracking the movements of the Cossack division across the landscape. They are now certain that Dolmachev is heading for Tavoos Goli and they are excited. Whenever they have occasion to mention Mullah Mir Hashem, they speak of him venomously and with much hostility. They are now ready to return to base and give Rahim Khan the advance warning. They fervently hope that nothing happens to make the general change course.

THIRTY-EIGHT

The Alarlus reached Sheytan Darreh refuge before sundown. There was a chill in the air redolent with the smell of autumn and ripening wild blackberries. The herds were ensconced in the safety of the crannies inside the dark valley. The men, individually or in groups, poked their sticks in the small springs flowing from under the boulders on the valley floor in hopes of increasing the water flow. The effort yielded mixed results. Success was followed by hoots and hollers and failure by resigned silence.

The patriarch, Hajji Ildrum, squatting on a goatskin mat, was smoking a water pipe, occasionally dipping a finger in bowl of water to remove the dust from around his eyes. The communal thirst had now been slaked and the camp was settling down for a restful night when the strange nocturnal rodents with large heads emerged from their warrens. Speedily, they spread up and down the valley, disturbing women and children in the tents and startling the sheep in their makeshift folds. The men rushed around chasing the creatures, crushing as many of them as they could with their clubs, trying mightily to settle down the frightened livestock. But then a sound, as of a loud peel of laughter, echoed from the dark end of the valley. All of a sudden, the rodents were nowhere to be seen as if they had retracted to their underground lair on cue. A stunned silence fell upon the camp.

Hajji Ildrum, bewildered and frustrated, was standing in the middle of all the commotion trying to get some kind of control. Now the men started to gather around him and a couple of them lit a bonfire with an armful of thistle. In its glow, Hajji looked around and asked, "What the hell was that?"

The Cannon

"What else, but a bunch of fucking mice running all over the valley frightening the livestock," a herder in the back row chimed in.

"They weren't mice," said the man poking the fire. "They were more like kittens."

"But what are all these kittens doing in a desolate place like this?" said Hajji Ildrum derisively. "If they weren't kittens," retorted the man, "they weren't mice, either. Nobody's ever seen mice like that."

Another herder came forward through men. He held by the tail a dead animal that in the light of the bonfire looked like an oversized rat with long but rounded claws and a large, woolly head dangling from a fleshy hairless body. A broad, red tongue was hanging out of its open mouth.

"Now what do you want me to do with this filthy thing?" asked Hajji in disgust. "I just thought you might want to see if it is a mouse or a cat," said the man, visibly miffed.

"Just throw it away," ordered Hajji Ildrum, "whatever fucking thing it is, you idiot." The herder turned around and disappeared in the darkness.

"I wanted to talk to you about what to do tomorrow," said Hajji Ildrum, "But as you saw we were distracted."

"They really caused a chaos, Hajji," said the tribal elder, unwilling to let go. "It's a mystery where they came from and where they went."

"I hope they won't come back tomorrow," intoned another man. "Hard to get the herds going if they are riled up like they were tonight."

"So, do you want me to find their holes and kill them all?" Hajji Ildrum, yelled, impatient and anxious to change the subject.

The company fell silent at Hajji's outburst. "All this hardship that has befallen us," said Hajji in a more conciliatory tone, "is that damned Mullah Hashem's fault."

"It is not all his fault, Khan," said a man from the back row. "There are also those sons of bitches Rahim Khan of Ghujabeglu and Havar Khan, not to mention that motherfucker the Cossack general."

"Right, but we could have dealt with each them," Hajji responded, "without suffering as much we are suffering now."

One of the men who was keeping the fire going raised his hand for permission to speak. "Be that as it may, Khan" he said, "let's think of something to do now."

"Not much to think about," Hajji Ildrum answered. "We have to trek back toward Ziveh, hoping that our adversaries have gone in the direction of Limlu valley."

"What if they haven't?" asked another. "I don't know," said Hajji Ildrum, irritated. "We'll cross that bridge when we come to it."

"But isn't it better to have a plan already, just in case" persisted the man.

"No," snapped Hajji Ildrum. "We can't make plans when we have no idea what lies ahead."

The congregation fell silent and only the sound of small rivulets flowing over the rocks could be heard.

"Now go get some sleep," commanded Hajji. "We've got a big day ahead of us tomorrow starting at sunrise."

Soon the camp was in total silence as the night dragged itself over the surrounding hills drowning all in darkness. Within hours the darkness was diluted with bland strains of light and soon the first rays of the sun hit the tips of the blackberry bushes on the crest of the hills.

The Cannon

Suddenly a high-pitched yell pierced the silence of the narrow valley: "Hey, hey, Hajji Ildrum!" No response came from the sleepy camp. But with the second call, several men burst out of the tents and started to look around in alarm.

On the brow of the hill facing them there were several Ghujabeglu horsemen. They had dismounted and were surveying the camp. They looked benign and unthreatening.

THIRTY-NINE

At the foot of the hills surrounding Tavoos Goli the column came to a halt. Dolmachev, Rahim Oghlu, and four of the junior officers congregated at a distance from the troops. Mullah Hashem, left by himself at the head of the column, was in the grip of fear and excruciating anxiety. The order had gone out to cut down on noise level to avoid alerting the adversary beyond the hills. All eyes were on Dolmachev in anticipation of new orders. Soon Rahim Oghlu returned with the order to dismount. Two Cossacks, from the middle of the column stepped forward with Dolmachev's armchair. The word was passed around that dinner would be served before sunset. The troops were then to take up positions on top of a hill covering the Tavoos Goli meadowland below.

As the men lined up by the chuck wagons, Rahim Oghlu carried Dolmachev's dinner tray to where he sat in the armchair. When he returned, he saw the mullah squatting on the ground deep in thought. "Have a bite," he said to the mullah.

"I'm not hungry. Don't feel like eating," the mullah said. Rahim Oghlu noticed the troubled look on the mullah's face. "Why not?" he asked. "You haven't had a thing to eat all day."

The mullah, distant and dismissive, said, "Oh, I just have no appetite." Rahim Oghlu had his mouth full. "I, on the contrary," he mumbled, "am starved."

"Then enjoy your dinner," said the mullah, trying to be pleasant. But Rahim Oghlu did not want to give up. "Mullah, you look distracted," he said. "What's the matter with you?"

"Nothing really," answered the mullah. "I just feel a bit depressed." He then turned and looked a Rahim Oghlu quizzically.

The Cannon

"I just wanted ..." he started but did not finish the sentence. "Wanted what?" asked Rahim Oghlu.

"I wanted to ask you," said the mullah, "what would the general do if he comes face to face with Rahim Khan?"

"Nothing," Rahim Oghlu chuckled with amusement. "He'll just hug him and kiss him and give him a pat on the back," Rahim Oghlu said sarcastically. "What a stupid question," he went on. "Of course he'll tear him apart."

"But why?" the mullah wanted to know.

"Because he has mutinied against the government," explained Rahim Oghlu. "If he hadn't done that, the general would not have bothered him."

"What is he going to hit him with?" asked the mullah.

"With everything he's got," Rahim Oghlu responded, still amused. "His weapons, his men, everything."

"Is he going to hit Rahim Khan only or anyone who's with him?" Rahim Oghlu stopped chewing and looked at the mullah, as if astonished by his naïveté. "In war you are not facing only one person. Everyone involved is likely to get hurt."

"What about the cannon?" the mullah asked. "Do you fire the cannon when you come across them?"

"Do you really want to know?" Rahim Oghlu queried. "Of course," said the mullah emphatically. "If you really want to know," Rahim Oghlu said, "then the answer is yes."

"But then you kill everyone," the mullah uttered in disbelief. "Hopefully," returned Rahim Oghlu, with a laugh.

"You kill everyone and everything within range, don't you?" said the mullah, horrified, "Even the sheep?"

"We don't kill anyone," said Rahim Oghlu with mock patience, as if talking to a child. "It is the artillery shell fired at the general's orders. The shrapnel has no eyes to see whom to hit or not. It simply does what it is supposed to do."

"But that is reprehensible," the mullah added. "Those innocent women and children and animals. They are not at fault."

"You don't understand, Mullah," Rahim Oghlu muttered as he chewed his food. "You don't think about these things in war."

"Can we do something else?" the mullah said speculatively. "Such as what?" Rahim Oghlu wanted to know. "Do something to change the general's plans," suggested the mullah. Perplexed, Rahim Oghlu asked, "What do you mean by change his plans?"

"To leave these poor, innocent people alone and not to shed their blood," said the mullah in a plaintiff tone. "What does he have against them?"

"Personally, he has nothing against them," Rahim Oghlu explained, as if to a child. "But he can't just get up and leave. He is here under orders and that is his mission."

"Why can't he just take it out on Rahim Khan and not use the cannon to slaughter women and children—and livestock?" the mullah said suggested. "This cannon is blind and cruel and kills indiscriminately," he added as an afterthought.

By now Rahim Oghlu's patience was wearing thin. He moved close to the mullah and stared him directly in the face. "It is not in your place to meddle in the general's business," he said ominously. "Do you know what he'll do to you if finds out the way you talk?"

The mullah, feeling admonished, lowered his eyes and remained quiet. Rahim Oghlu relented and said in a conciliatory tone, "Listen, what is it that you're afraid of? Why are you so concerned? You are safe."

The Cannon

"I'm afraid for those innocent lives," the mullah whined. "I'm scared of the cannon and how cruel it can be."

Patronizingly, Rahim Oghlu addressed the mullah: "Come now, don't be scared. You have never seen it up close. Come with me and I'll show you what a beautiful piece of work it is."

Rahim Oghlu finished his meal, reached out to help the mullah to his feet as they headed for the far end of the camp where the cannon had been parked. As they approached it, a deep, visceral fear gripped the mullah. Reflexively, he wrapped his cloak around him. As if approaching a living monster, he feared that at any moment it might reach out and snatch him with its claws.

When they reached the vicinity of the cannon, Rahim Oghlu said, "Now, Mullah, look at it," making an expansive gesture with his hand. "See, it is not scary at all."

The mullah gazed in awe first at the outsized wheels of the carriage and then at the long polished barrel pointed skyward, as if staring at an indefinite point in deep space. Rahim Oghlu, stroking the smooth barrel admiringly, said, "Are you still scared? Ha?"

The mullah wrapped himself tighter in his cloak. "No wonder it scares me. It looks so cruel, so ferocious," he whimpered.

FORTY

By mid-afternoon, as the general had ordered, the cannon had been pulled up to the pathway that ascended to a narrow pass before heading steeply down the other side to the Tavoos Goli grasslands. The gunner, supervising the process, checked the harnesses tying the team of mules to the gun carriage and nodded his satisfaction to Dolmachev. At that point Dolmachev ordered his officers to divide the column in four defensive formations and start the climb toward the pass with himself in the company of Rahim Oghlu and the mullah, who kept himself at a distant from the other two, leading the forward squad. There sound of the movement of men and footfalls of horses was uncannily muted. The men, nervous in anticipation of impending action, restrained their horses as they advanced cautiously up the hill when suddenly Dolmachev raised his hand. The contingent came to an instantaneous halt. Holding their breath, the men watched as Rahim Oghlu dismounted, fell to his knees, took his carbine off his back, and started to crawl with practiced agility toward the ridge. The men watched intently, waiting for Rahim Oghlu's assessment of the situation. The mullah, his heart palpitating, prayed under his breath and kept looking around as if for an exit.

Rahim Oghlu stopped when he was near the top. Slowly, he raised his head and for what seemed like an eternity surveyed the valley. He rose to his feet and, legs apart, gazed ahead. The men held their rifles at the ready for a possible raid. Rahim Oghlu then turned around and started walking toward Dolmachev as he slung his weapon over his shoulder. "Hey, Rahim Oghlu, what's going on?" yelled Dolmachev in exasperation. Rahim Oghlu extended his arms, showing the palms off his hands as he shook his head, an all-clear gesture. Dolmachev

The Cannon

spurred his horse and took off in a gallop toward the ridge, followed by the Cossacks who rushed after him helter-skelter. When they reached the top what they saw before them was the Tavoos Goli valley, flanked on either side by ranges of hills of varying height and seasonally yellowing grass carpeting the valley floor with a few black spots here and there indicating where the campfires had been. There was no sign of life anywhere.

"Hey, Mullah," roared Dolmachev.

All eyes turned to the mullah. Rahim Oghlu beckoned to him to come forward. The mullah, holding tightly to his furled banner, as if a talisman against harm, rode ahead, the troops opening a narrow passage for him. When he reached Dolmachev and saw that the valley was deserted, he turned pale with a combination of anxiety and relief.

"Mullah," barked Dolmachev, "where are the Ghujabeglus?"

"They aren't gone," answer the mullah redundantly. "They must have left before we got here."

"But gone where?" Dolmachev asked, his face flushed. "I don't know, General," the mullah said. "God only knows."

"Didn't you lead us along the migration trail?" asked Dolmachev, clearly annoyed. "But I did, General," answered the mullah earnestly. "We came along the Gharagun Trail. It is the main migratory trail of the Ghujabeglus."

"So, why didn't we run into them?" asked Dolmachev accusingly. "Perhaps they have taken a detour," answered the mullah. "What detour?" snapped Dolmachev.

The mullah hesitated a moment and then explained haltingly that detours have no names or a specific routes and that he could not possibly have known the path taken by Rahim Khan and his clan. He was repeatedly interrupted by Dolmachev who was increasingly contentious and accusatory. "So if you weren't sure what path the Ghujabeglus have taken, why did you lead us to this damned spot?" he wanted to know. "Just a few days ago they were here," the mullah explained.

"How do you know they were here?" Dolmachev asked, his eyes narrowed with suspicion. "How do I know you are not lying to me? How do I know you did not lead us astray?"

"I wouldn't do that, General," the mullah pleaded. "I recited the laments for them down there," he said, vaguely pointing to a spot nearby. "I delivered a sermon in the consecrated tent."

Looking grim, Dolmachev turned to Rahim Oghlu. "What do we do now?" he asked, not really expecting an answer.

"We can't do much right now," Rahim Oghlu answered. "The light is failing and we'd better prepare to settle down for the night and plan for tomorrow."

"I'll send a dispatch to General Federov tomorrow," announced Dolmachev, "to tell him we can't do much in this hell hole. He'd better think of another strategy."

He then faced Mullah Mir Hashem. "And if you have lied to us," he said darkly, "first thing in the morning, I'll have you tied to a horse and dragged all over the valley. That'll teach you a lesson." The mullah pursed his lips and said nothing.

Rahim Oghlu ordered two Cossacks to go back to the gunner and tell him to be ready next morning to haul the cannon over into the valley. At Dolmachev's command the Cossacks streamed down the hillside.

FORTY-ONE

At sunrise a troop of nearly forty Cossacks were clearing the way to move the cannon over the hills into Tavoos Goli valley. The cannon had already been harnessed to a team of well-fed, well-rested mules. As the animals strained against the load, some men were leaning their shoulders against the wheels of the gun carriage pushing it forward .... The advance over the uneven and rocky pathway was rough and convulsive, the huge cannon rocking perilously in all directions as it was pushed forward. Rahim Oghlu and the gunner, walking side-by-side, gave occasional directions to the crew.

"Rahim Oghlu," said the gunner, "now that there is nothing going on, why do we have to haul this thing over to the valley?"

"It is not up to us," replied Rahim Oghlu. "It is the general's orders." But the gunner was not satisfied. "In my reckoning," he said, "it is going to take more than a day to get the damned thing over the hill." Clearly, Rahim Oghlu not willing to pursue the conversation in this vein. "It's not for us to say," he said curtly, "We're here only to follow orders." Ignoring him, the gunner pursued the matter. "What if something breaks and we get bogged down here?" he asked, sounding genuinely concerned.

"Then it is out of our hands. It'll be all up to the general," Rahim Oghlu said to bring the discussion to an end.

By now the progress had become even more tortuous and labored. The men with their shoulders to the wheels and the mules pulling strenuously against the harness were panting heavily and seemed almost out of breath. Rahim Oghlu and the gunner flailed their whips over their heads and, as if to release their frustration, kept cursing the men and whipping the mules.

FORTY-TWO

In the middle of the public square of the hamlet a pulpit had been set up and a large crowd of people representing almost all the clans in the region were standing around, waiting impatiently to hear Mullah Imamverdi Meshkini who had just arrived from Tabriz, the provincial capital with fresh news. The noise died down when he ascended the pulpit and began to announce his message with a loud and clear voice, a message that would soon carry from village to village and town to town in the territory.

"People," Mullah Imamverdi bellowed, "this time I have good news for you. With the blessing of God Almighty the Mojahedin,* taking their lives in their hands on behalf of our nation, have pushed away the government forces from the walls of the city. This would not have been possible without the efforts of volunteer riflemen from your area. I am here to tell you, people, that there is yet more work to do …."

The oration echoed everywhere in the village and beyond, galvanizing the clans to action. By the end of the day squads of armed men, led by Mullah Imamverdi, were galloping across the hills and plains in the direction of the capital city.

---

* The paramilitary arm of the Constitutionalists in the Iranian Constitutional Movement, 1906-1911.

FORTY-THREE

The news of Dolmachev's arrival in Tavoos Goli spread all over the Shahsevan territory like wildfire. More than anything else, Rahim Khan and his men were instrumental in carrying the news to tribal chiefs and clan leaders. All of a sudden, all feuds, rivalries, and enmities were set aside in the face of a clear and present danger. Preparations got underway to counter the common enemy in Tavoos Goli.

The Ghujabeglus had changed their course on their way to the winter camp and had taken a detour to intercept the Cossack division in case Dolmachev decided to retreat from Tavoos Goli. Meanwhile, Rahim Khan and his aide Uzun had enlisted five other khans and formed a sizeable expeditionary force and were advancing in the direction of Tavoos Goli. Rahim Khan's single artillery piece, a field gun drawn by four mules and escorted by several men, brought up the rear. Men from Hajjikhujalu and Alarlu tribes, with no traces of animosity between them had converged on the Ziveh hillside, broken bread together, and were now planning a joint strategy to deal with the common enemy.

Similar scenes were in progress all over the landscape in the tribal region. Women, children, and the livestock had been dispatched to wintering areas away from imminent danger and the men were congregating at various locations in a spirit of solidarity to dispel a mutual foe. All instruments of war had been distributed among able-bodied men. Some who did not have weapons were carrying slingshots, shovels, clubs, and rocks. The Damirchlu tribesmen, for example, who traditionally never carried weapons, had brought with them containers of black tar. They were experts in making great balls of fire by dousing bundles of thistle with black tar and rolling them down the hill to disrupt enemy formation.

FORTY-FOUR

At dawn two heavy-set Cossacks brought Mullah Mir Hashem out of Sha'ban's tent and led him to Dolmachev's quarters. The air was chillier now and tiny dewdrops on the soft grass sparkled in the early sunlight. The contingent had already been deployed at the western end of the plain. The kitchen was in full operation and some Cossacks had lined up before its black tent. The huge gun had been set up on a flat surface and its long barrel was raised at an angle aiming at an indeterminate target.

Earlier that morning, Dolmachev and Rahim Oghlu had observed the surrounding terrain. Dolmachev had returned upset and apprehensive. He had had his breakfast and now sent for the mullah. Outside the general's tent Rahim Oghlu waited, horsewhip in hand. He stepped forward to meet the mullah. "Hey, Mullah, Dolmachev is really mad at you," he warned. "If you want to live, answer his questions truthfully."

"What does the general want to know?" asked the mullah, alarmed.

"I don't know what he wants to ask you, but I know one thing," Rahim Oghlu said knowingly, "that he has a feeling that you've tricked him and brought him here for the wrong reason. Should this be the case," Rahim Oghlu advised, "you'd be better off to fess up and throw yourself on his mercy."

The mullah, apoplectic with fright, swore a string of inarticulate oaths protesting his innocence when Rahim Oghlu raised his hand, cutting him off in mid-sentence. "Don't swear for me. Save all that for the general," he said, as he pushed the mullah through the curtains into the tent.

Inside the tent Dolmachev was seated on a bench surrounded by nearly a dozen dogs in bright, metal collars and wildly

The Cannon

gleaming eyes. From an air vent on the top of the tent a shaft of sunlight had illumined a circle of light at Dolmachev's feet with a white, furry dog warming itself in its middle. Dolmachev stood up as the mullah was pushed into the tent.

"Hey, Mullah, it's high time I cut off your head and shoved it into your guts," hissed Dolmachev, shaking his whip at the man. "That'll teach you not to fool around with General Dolmachev." Glancing apprehensively at the dogs, now glaring alarmingly at him, the mullah whimpered, "I have done nothing wrong, General."

"So," barked Dolmachev, "where on earth is this place you got us into?" The mullah answered, "It's Tavoos Goli, the Ghujabeglus summer camp, General." Frustrated and with his voice rising in anger, Dolmachev asked, "So where the hell are they themselves?" The mullah, scared and sheepish, replied, "I don't know. They must have left before we arrived." He then continued, with a tinge of hope in his voice, "If it pleases the General, I can go find out where they are. Perhaps in another summering camp farther."

"It is that simple, huh?" Dolmachev said sarcastically. He got up and, tapping the mullah's forehead with the handle of the whip, continued: "I am not going to fall for it this time. You think you can trick me again and get away from me that easy?" Trying to muster as much sincerity as possible in his voice, the mullah protested, "I am not trying to get away. I am not lying. I haven't tricked you, General. Never." Unimpressed, Dolmachev retorted, fuming, "So why are we in this hell hole, in the middle of nowhere?" He then struck the mullah in the face with the whip. The mullah, distraught and desperate, sank to the floor, rubbing his face. The dogs rose, as if on cue, and made way for Dolmachev to step back from the mullah.

"Be ashamed of yourself, you lying bastard!" Dolmachev screamed. "What am I going to do with you?" he asked rhetorically. Covering his face with his hands, the mullah pleaded in a muffled voice, "Let me go and get you the right information, General. If you don't trust me, send a Cossack with me."

Ignoring the mullah, Dolmachev stomped toward the opening of the tent and called for Rahim Oghlu, who appeared instantly and stood at attention just inside the tent.

"Hey, Cossack," Dolmachev ordered, "take this piece of shit outside and have a heart-to-heart with him to see what he really is up to. If he is still evasive and reluctant to talk, scalp him. And if that didn't work, go ahead and waste a bullet on him."

As if delighted with his mission, Rahim Oghlu, grabbed the mullah by the scruff of his neck and yanked him to his feet, dragging him out of the tent.

FORTY-FIVE

At nightfall, Rahim Khan, Havar Khan, and Hajji Ildrum had congregated with their lieutenants in a huge tent. By order of Rahim Khan several lambs had been slaughtered and were being roasted on an open fire in front of the tent. Uzun, Rahim Khan's special chef, kept a constant supply of roasted meat carried to the tent on big copper trays.

The three tribal leaders, sharing their evening meal, voraciously bit into the pieces of meat and kept a jovial conversation going. As he salted a dripping cut of lamb in his bare hands, Rahim Khan addressed his peers: "Now is the time to set aside ancient quarrels and unite against this mother-fucker Dolmachev and see what happens afterwards." In a spirit of solidarity, Hajji Ildrum agreed, adding, "Once we have accomplished that, we will just continue to live in peace and go our own way. Nothing untoward will happen."

"Aside from future peace and harmony," Havar Khan chimed in, "it is imperative that we dispose of Dolmachev and his troops—and that cannon of his. Until that is achieved we cannot rest." In addition to the cannon, and Dolmachev and his troops, we will also be rid of that son of a bitch Mullah Mir Hashem. Now that he's been exposed, he can't trick us any more.

"I just can't believe he's such a vermin," said Hajji Ildrum bitterly.

"My men saw with their own eyes the mullah walking side-by-side with Dolmachev," added Rahim Khan. "They trailed them all the way to Tavoos Goli." He went on solemnly, "The time of reckoning is at hand."

"I believe that," said Havar Khan. "You can't imagine the damage he's done to us." Hajji Ildrum and Rahim Khan both said things to the same effect and all three expressed satisfaction at the mullah's ultimate exposure.

"What I don't understand," said Hajji Ildrum, his eyes narrowed to a slit, "is why he should betray us like that. We never did him any harm and my folks always treated him with proper respect for his calling, and we've broken bread together many times."

"Over the years, he has amassed a herd of nearly three hundred heads of sheep with our tribe," Havar Khan informed the other men.

"I divvied up his herd among his shepherds the other day," added Rahim Khan.

"You did the right thing," said Havar Khan approvingly. "I'll do the same first chance I get."

"But wait a minute," interrupted Hajji Ildrum with some reservation.

"What for?" retorted Rahim Khan. "What he's done has lost him the sanctity* both of his life and his property. Wait until we get a hold of him."

"I really want to have a man-to-man talk with him," said Havar Khan.

"No use talking to him," Rahim Khan said dismissively. "He's past redemption."

"Do you think he'll deny he's done anything wrong?" Havar Khan wanted to know.

"I don't even want to think what he'll do," Rahim Khan said disgustedly. "I believe we should just deal with him as soon as we get him."

---

*In Islamic law, the property of the accused is beyond the reach of civil authority.

The Cannon

"What do you mean 'deal with him'?" asked Hajji Ildrum.

"Just put a bullet through his head," replied Rahim Khan.

"That lets him off too easy," objected Havar Khan. "We should take more drastic measures, to make an example of him, teach others a lesson."

"What if we decapitate him and put his head on display on his chest?" ruminated Rahim Khan.

"We must make as wide a spectacle of that as possible," suggested Havar Khan.

"What about dragging him behind a horse?" asked Rahim Khan, as if he had come up with the final solution. "But that finishes him off too fast," answered Havar Khan. "He should suffer more."

"We should cut him to pieces," said Rahim Khan sadistically, "and put each piece on display in strategic spots all over the valley for all to see. How about that?"

The other men chuckled, as if amused by the Khan's rancor. To change the subject, Hajji Ildrum asked, "What about Dolmachev? What should we do with him?"

"Nothing," ejaculated Rahim Khan, to the surprise of the other two. "Nothing? Why not?" asked Hajji Ildrum.

"No," Rahim Khan stressed. "We do nothing to him and his Cossacks. We will leave them an escape route so they can beat a hasty retreat."

"But isn't he the one that invaded our territory?" challenged Havar Khan, "and brought that great gun to do us harm?"

Calmly, Rahim Khan went on, "if we start the slaughter, they will send more troops and bigger guns and before we know it we'll all be exterminated."

"So, there will be no battles, no engagement with the Cossack Division?" asked Hajji Ildrum, as if relieved.

"We have coordinated the tribes," explained Rahim Khan. "We can stage a surprise attack pouring into the valley from three sides and leave the north tribal migration path open. This will leave them no choice but to retreat that way helter-skelter. In the commotion, we will capture the gun and Mullah Mir Hashem. And that will be that."

Hajji Ildrum and Havar Khan glanced at each other, tacitly approving the strategy. Rahim Khan turned his head toward the tent entrance. "Hey, Uzun," he thundered. As if expecting the call, Uzun entered the tent carrying a large tray piled high with steaming roasted meat. The khans set upon the tray with ravenous appetite.

FORTY-SIX

At dusk Dolmachev had ordered Rahim Oghlu to come to his tent with paper and pen to take down a letter. Rahim Oghlu stood at attention near the entrance ready for the dictation. Overstuffed and distended with a heavy evening meal and still feeling the buzz of the dinner wine, Dolmachev was pacing the floor of the tent. A troubled and pained look was on his face and as soon as he began the dictation, it degenerated into a rant, a griping monologue, betraying his frustration and disappointment.

"Write this down," he barked at Rahim Oghlu, "Hey, General Federov, in this god-forsaken place no one can do anything. These highland sierras are endless, one range of hills after another. It is not clear why we are here or what we are supposed to do or whom to fight with. After a month of wandering around, we haven't encountered a single soul. The Ghujabeglus went back on their word and refused to cooperate. I am now chasing them all over the place trying to catch them and teach them a lesson. But to no avail. They're nowhere to be found. Think of something else, General Federov."

As if out of breath, Dolmachev paused. "Write this down," he started again, "The Cossacks can't stay here indefinitely. The highlands are getting cold and I don't know if I should move back down to the plains. No way to know where the hell these sons of bitches are hiding. None of these fucking pimps is willing to help. They're all mother-fucker bastards. We thought we had a promising lead when a mullah, a cleric, agreed to collaborate. But he also played a trick on us and got us roaming the empty range for the past ten days. I wish you were here to see how ridiculous he looks. A handful of skin and bones with full, heavy beard, in an old, tattered tunic. But, General Federov, he is some piece of work!"

Dolmachev now sank in the armchair, exhausted with the exertion. "Hey, Rahim Oghlu, time to tend to the mullah," he said, almost gleefully. "You can write Federov's letter later. Tell them to bring him in." Rahim Oghlu left the tent momentarily to execute the order. When he returned, Dolmachev asked, absent-mindedly almost, playing with his fingers, "What shall we do with him, do you think?"

"Whatever is the General's pleasure," replied Rahim Oghlu, sensing the general's mood.

"I really want to let him have it," the general said, still contemplating his fingers.

"That is very appropriate, Sir."

"I want to shoot him between the eyes. How about that?"

"Great idea, General."

"This way, he won't suffer enough, though."

"So, the General will think of some other way."

"How about tying him to two horses and dragging him over the landscape?"

"This is also a good idea, Sir."

"You realize that he has lied to us and got us on the wrong track, hasn't he?"

"Yes, Sir."

"I'll order the regimental cook to cut off his tongue."

"I am very much in favor of this."

"I'm afraid that he'll succumb and die too soon."

"That's a distinct possibility, Sir."

"But I want to play with him, have a little fun."

"That will be very good, Sir."

The Cannon

"For instance," Dolmachev said, as if thinking aloud, "I'll get him drunk first. Then I'll have him wrapped in a blanket. And then I'll roll him down a steep hill."

"That will be great," replied Rahim Oghlu, appearing to be enthusiastic. "This is a lot of fun."

At this point, two Cossacks delivered the mullah at the tent entrance. Rahim Oghlu dismissed the soldiers and turned to Mullah Hashem, who looked incredibly emaciated. He had spent the past two days in a small tent in chains without food or water. He could barely walk and his chin trembled visibly. "Sit down," commanded Dolmachev. The mullah collapsed on the throw rug before Rahim Oghlu.

"I've heard," said Dolmachev jovially, "you've been having a good time these past two days."

"Thank God," the mullah muttered, reflexively.

"Whether or not you confess, we are convinced of your treachery, your ploy to lead us astray. Now is the time of reckoning, time for you to be dealt your deserts," said Dolmachev pompously. "But I am a fair-minded man. I will let you choose your own punishment. Here are your options … send you to your Maker with this pistol, or have your tongue cut out, slowly, painfully … or have you dragged behind horses in a rocky field. Or, you can spare yourself all the pain by drinking from this jug."

The mullah asked weakly, "What is in the jug?"

"Wine," announced Dolmachev resoundingly.

The mullah looked at the two men, plaintively, despondently. "I can't, General," he said tremulously. "I've never ingested sanctioned substances."

"What happens if you do?" Dolmachev wanted to know.

"This is forbidden. I can't drink it."

"But if I demand it, you have to."

"Please, General, make another demand. I have spent a lifetime reciting the praise of Imam Ali and his progeny. It is an abomination to partake of this libation."

"What about the pistol? That is not an abomination, is it?"

"I am sick, I am stricken, General. Have mercy on me and let me go."

Dolmachev paused for a moment and then said coldly and with deliberation: "Not this time, not any more. It is either the pistol or the wine. Which one do you like better? Huh, which one is your preference?"

"I … I … can't … General … I … I … haven't … haven't done anything … Please …," the mullah stuttered.

"He doesn't know what is in his best interest," said Dolmachev, turning to Rahim Oghlu. "Pour some of that 'abomination' down his throat." Rahim Oghlu picked up the jug and walked in the direction of the mullah. Writhing with fear on the floor, the mullah had grabbed the throw rug, pressing it against his chest, as if hoping to hide behind it. Rahim Oghlu pushed him flat on his back, placed his left knee on his chest to immobilize him, and with his left hand pressed on both sides of the mullah's face, forced open his mouth. Just as he brought the jug forward toward the mullah's mouth a tremendous yell shook the tent.

"What the hell!" yelped Dolmachev.

Involuntarily, Rahim Oghlu sprang up off the mullah and in the direction of the tent entrance, followed closely by Dolmachev.

In what seemed like a flash flood, streams of tribesmen, armed with shovels, rakes, and clubs were rushing down the sides of the surrounding hill toward the encampment yelling at the top of their voices.

FORTY-SEVEN

Under the silvery light of the moon brightening the Tavoos Goli valley, General Dolmachev's great cannon lay inert like a sleeping giant, unaware of numberless men, bedraggled, disorderly, who were hastening to reach it on its perch at the far end of the valley. The commotion was exacerbated by Dolmachev's men, who had been startled out of sleep and out of their tents by the onslaught of the tribesmen, and were milling around, some unarmed, others carrying their weapons, aimless and disoriented, howling, cursing, and running into each other. Most were looking at Dolmachev's tent on the prominent brow of a hill for orders on how to proceed. However, before any orders or a sign of a central command emerged from the tent, the tribesmen had surrounded the cannon and set the surprised gun crew in flight. The neighing of horses added to the commotion as some tribesmen mounted the gun and from atop its barrel were yelling "Escape! Escape!" causing further confusion among the Cossacks who could not find any signs of their commanders.

Surprisingly, no weapons were being discharged, despite threatening gestures and posturing on both sides. The Cossacks, disoriented and in disarray, pressed Rahim Oghlu for orders to some action. At a corner of the camp flames could be seen rising from a burning tent, the only emanation of hostile action by the invaders, although the flow of men armed in clubs and sticks streaming down the hills seemed interminable, adding by the minute the congestion inside the valley.

FORTY-EIGHT

Dolmachev and Rahim Oghlu stood at the tent entrance transfixed by the scene of chaos and pandemonium spread before them all the way to the surrounding hills. All of a sudden out of nowhere Rahim Khan, Havar Khan, and Hajji Ildrum appeared before them, each with his rifle at the ready aiming directly at their chests. Incredulous and shaken by the nightmarish spectacle before him, Dolmachev took a step backward into the tent, but before Rahim Oghlu could make a similar move, he was immobilized by Rahim Khan's roar: "One move out of you and I'll riddle you with bullets, I swear!"

An old oil lamp cast a forlorn light on the two captives as they stood just barely inside the tent watched closely by the tribesmen. Mullah Mir Hashem, who was slowly recovering from his ordeal, jumped to his feet, elated by the altered circumstances. "Hey, Khan, here I am," he screeched with unbounded delight. "Praised be my Holy Ancestors[*] for sending you to my rescue!" He opened his arms, uncertain which one of the khans to embrace first. Rahim Khan stepped forward toward him, but before he could say anything, Havar Khan raised the butt of his rifle, and with it hit the mullah in the chest, sprawling him on his back on the floor. "Mother-fucker!" he said disgustedly.

Standing at the tent entrance, Rahim Khan spoke. His tone was solemn and formal. "General Dolmachev," he began. "I am Rahim Khan of the Ghujabeglus. You are now a prisoner of twenty-two Shahsevan tribes. We outnumber your Cossack Regiment ten to one. But we are offering you amnesty if your order a withdrawal of your troops. If not we are ready to deal

---

[*] As a cleric, the mullah claims a direct line of descent to Prophet Mohammad.

The Cannon

with them, and with you yourself before anyone else. Right here and now." What followed was a terse, staccato dialogue between the two men. "Hey man, this insurgency is going to cost you dear," said Dolmachev with a trace of defiance in his voice. "Insurgency? What insurgency and against whom?" shot back Rahim Khan.

"You're disobeying the direct orders of your government."

"I am not a subject of the government to obey its orders."

"But you had made an agreement to pacify the tribes."

"My agreements are no concern of yours and your superiors. You have no business to invade the tribal region."

"My mission is to assist you in your efforts."

"I need no assistance."

"You were not up to what you were supposed to do single-handedly."

"Once again, that is not your business."

"I did not come here of my own accord. I am carrying out General Federov's orders."

"I did tell you right off to turn around and go back to where you came from."

"But I wanted to expedite things."

"And the first thing to expedite was my demise, wasn't it?"

"You did not heed my advice. You did not show me the way. You did not assist me in my mission. You simply told me to turn around and go back. Don't you understand that I cannot take orders except from General Federov?"

"I am now the one ordering you to take your unit and leave."

"It is not that simple."

"It is simpler than you think."

"What shall I tell General Federov?"

"It is up to you. You can begin by telling him that we seized your artillery piece and sent you packing."

At this point Havar Khan interjected: "Yes, General Dolmachev, your prized artillery piece is now in our possession. You give us any trouble and we will turn it on you. We want no other trophies but, first, the cannon and, second, this son of a bitch of a mullah."

Hajji Ildrum, who had been silent so far, said impatiently, "All right, don't haggle with him. It is getting late." Rahim Khan, turning to Dolmachev, said, "Now, order your men to move. Any of your elements still here after an hour will not be immune." Dolmachev, addressing Rahim Oghlu, muttered, "Hey Cossack, go give orders to decamp." Rahim Oghlu moved away from the group and disappeared in the gathering darkness. Havar Khan moved toward the mullah and grabbed him by the collar of his cowl. "You unholy dog," he said, gazing directly into the mullah's eyes, "You see where we got you? Now you can't deny anything."

FORTY-NINE

By first light, at the foot of a high hill on the Gharagul migratory trail, the order had been given for a brief rest after the nightlong trek. A bitingly cold breeze was blowing and the yellow-tinged grass of early autumn was covered with a crystalline patina of thin ice. The Cossacks had lined up before the chuck wagons in anticipation of leftovers from previous night's meal.

General Dolmachev, was ensconced in his armchair, a thick sheepskin blanket covering his legs. Rahim Oghlu, looking fatigued and haggard, was in attendance. "Hey Cossack, why did things turn out this way?" Dolmachev, thoughtful and crestfallen, asked Rahim Oghlu. "It is all the fault of that mullah," he answered. "He deceived us all. He wanted to get us all killed and the tribal chiefs to capture the gun."

"No, Cossack," said Dolmachev ruefully, "it is not his fault. It is my fault. It is your fault." Then, with a shake of the head indicating the men milling around the kitchen, he said vehemently, "It is the fault of those fat-assed good-for-nothings who can't do anything but stuff their guts every chance they get. I'll take it out on them, you'll see. Go ahead and sound the bugle to assemble."

Rahim Oghlu moved promptly and within seconds the bugle sounded and the Cossacks rushed toward horses hitched to boulders along the trail. Swinging his old swagger stick, Rahim Oghlu was directing the line-up for inspection. Some of the men were still chewing on their last mouthful. They all looked tired and were covered in dust. The gunner, with his red epaulettes that accentuated the droop of his shoulders, was on a mule at the end of the front line. He appeared apprehensive and tremulous. The bugle sounded again and Rahim Oglu called the order for attention. The men sat straight on their mounts. Dolmachev guided his horse forward to face the line of men who were holding their breath, not knowing what to expect.

"All present?" he asked at the top of his voice.

"All present and accounted for," replied Rahim Oghlu.

"Anyone sick, or wounded, or dead, or lost?"

"No, Sir. All hale and hearty," came the answer.

"Why are they all healthy? Why are there no injuries, no casualties, deaths?" asked Dolmachev. Rahim Oghlu was clearly lost for an answer. Dolmachev moved close to the ranks. This time addressing the men, he asked, "Didn't you have instructions on how to proceed?"

"Yes, Sir," came the answer from men in a harmonious shout.

"Why then did no one act accordingly? Why then did no one risk injury or death in the line of duty? So we came all this way just to lose the cannon to a bunch of worthless tribesmen! I'll let General Federov deal with you all," he bellowed wrathfully.

This time there was no answer.

"Read the command communiqué," Dolmachev ordered Rahim Oghlu, who began to recite from memory:

"By the General's orders there will be no malingering, indulging in excessive consumption of food and drink, or undue socializing and fraternizing among the troops. Slothfulness and gluttony will not be tolerated. All must obey the call to action and assiduously observe the chain of command in the field. The General has ordained that no one has the right to get killed. The General has ordered the column to move."

At the sound of the bugle, Dolmachev took up his position at the head of the regiment. As the column moved, a fine dust began to rise in its trail.

FIFTY

Three days later they arrived at the foot of the highest summit in the Gharachumagh range of hills. They hauled the gun to the base of the summit and positioned it on a ledge overlooking the valleys on either side of the range. Then they proceeded to secure it with rocks as dark and shiny as gunmetal. The gun had within range a vast tract of the surrounding plains that were studded with small settlements, their inhabitants now trekking in waves toward the assemblage of men working on the gun. Soon, under the faint rays of the autumn sun, they had gathered at the foot of the hill, gazing at the gigantic bulk of the cannon in amazement and awe. The weapon, as if a living behemoth, seemed to stretch its monstrous limbs after a long sleep.

Uzun and Abolfazl, with their work now completed, were leaning against the gun carriage chatting with seven or eight other young men, mostly griping about the beastly cold breeze. They could not help but notice that the surrounding fields were now covered with throngs of people wrapped in heavy shawls for protection against the freezing air.

The sun, now past the meridian, headed toward the western horizon covered in a band of dark clouds, not unlike gun smoke belched by numberless cannon and frozen in place in the distant sky.

The crowds below the hill continued to grow. Some had resorted to making huge piles of thistle and underbrush for bonfires to ward off the chill in the air. But the activities did not distract their unwavering attention to the main event of the day that was in progress in a large tent hitched on the brow of the hill near the gun emplacement. Inside the tent Rahim Khan, Hajji Ildrum, Havar Khan, and several Shahsevan graybeards had gathered to discuss the recent events and deliberate on the fate of Mullah Mir Hashem. When the wind occasionally blew aside the curtains at the tent entrance, those outside could catch a glimpse of the congregants and the mullah, who stood in the middle of the tent with his back to the entrance. Directly in front of him were Rahim Khan, Hajji Ildrum, Havar Khan, seated on the floor leaning against large cushions, puffing on a water pipe which they passed among them. Each one had a rifle on his lap.

By now a verdict had been reached. Rahim Khan took a prolonged puff on the pipe and rose to his feet, holding his rifle by the barrel, tapping its butt on the floor as he moved slowly and deliberately toward the mullah to face him. He stared into the mullah's face for a long moment and then reached and grabbed the man's ample beard in his fist. "It is all over now, Mullah," he said, his voice thick with bitterness and venom. "Hey, Khan, If you let me ...," the mullah began to say, but was interrupted as the khan rapidly moved his hand to cover his mouth. "Shut your trap," the khan yelled. "You have no right to speak. You have no right at all." Then, taking his hand off the man's mouth, he asked, "Do you know why?"

"No, Khan. If ..." the mullah tried to respond but was silenced by a rapid jab of the khan's fist. "Silence! Not a single word out of you!" the khan ordered, and took a few steps backward before moving toward the mullah again. "Do you remember where we found you?" asked the khan, and proceeded to give the answer: "In Dolmachev's tent, for God's sakes."

The mullah took one step forward and made another attempt: "You see, Khan," but was silenced by the man's menacing glare.

Havar Khan, who was watching the scene intently, gestured to the attendants standing just outside the tent. A few young men came in and took the mullah by his arms and walked him out of

The Cannon

the tent. The crowd outside fell silent at the sight of the mullah, staring at him in wonderment, as if he was an alien species, a creature from another world.

Mullah Mir Hashem, groggy and disoriented, raised his head and saw the gun with its barrel reaching into the sky, looking like a gargantuan wild beast, claws biting into the dirt, ready to pounce. Those who been in their tents came out to join the crowd. The volume of the hum of the crowd, in turn, increased. The young men accompanying the mullah pushed him forward. He felt almost detached from his surroundings, even from his own body. He barely sensed his feet dragging on the frosted ground and his arms flailing uselessly to give him balance in his slow progress. Just before the ascent to the gun position, the mullah was made to stop. A fat peasant with a cleft palate appeared carrying a heavy sack. With some exertion, he lifted it, placing it on the mullah's back. The mullah almost sank to the ground under its weight. Nevertheless, he held onto it uncomplaining and continued the walk up the slowly rising path toward the gun. The object in the sack felt rounded and metallic, pressing against his backbone and ribs, inflicting considerable pain and increasing the agony of his progress step by step. He was aware of the pressing crowds closing in on him on three sides, intent on getting a better view of him. But much to his surprise he was indifferent to them as he labored under the weight of his burden on his way up the hill. When he arrived at a flat part of the track, he stopped to catch his breath. But he resumed the walk as if impelled by an unknown and unknowable force. Somehow, he had a sense that the crowds and their hubbub were receding farther and farther away, affording him a space, a vacuum, which he found strangely pleasing. But the momentary serenity was breached by sharp bite of the cold wind and the total exhaustion that brought him to his knees and sent a shudder through his body. He could barely hear Rahim Khan shouting to his men, "Pull him up."

Now two men were holding him under each arm moving him forward. The mullah obstinately held on to the load on his back until they reached a spot where the men let go of him. He allowed the sack to roll off and drop to the ground with a thud. His feet collapsed under him and he fell prostrate under the barrel of the gun. Uzun stepped forward with long strides and untied the sack. A large artillery shell rolled out of it.

Rahim Khan, Hajji Ildrum, and Havar Khan came forward and touched the barrel of the gun. They laughed an involuntary, mirthless laugh. The mullah, now lifted from the ground and seated on the tail of the gun carriage, felt warm drops of sweat rolling down his spine. He wrapped his cowl close to him and looked at the jubilant crowd on the lower reaches of the hill. The noise they made reminded him of the footfalls of thousands of sheep following a tribe in migration. He smiled broadly.

The wind had now picked up and flapped the lapels of the men's outerwear noisily. The leaden evening clouds moved with alarming speed eastward, causing some apprehension in the crowds below the hilltop.

"Everything set?" asked Rahim Khan, addressing Uzun.

"I'm ready, Khan," Uzun replied.

"Did you give him water?"

"Not yet, Khan,"

Rahim Khan gestured to a jug nearby. Uzun picked it up and brought it up to touch the mullah's lips. The mullah took a sip and turned his head.

"Let's go ahead," Rahim Khan said grimly.

The Cannon

Uzun, helped by Abolfazl, lifted the artillery shell off the ground and carefully loaded it into the gun's magazine. He cocked the firing mechanism before walking toward the mullah.

"Take the damned turban off his head," Rahim Khan ordered dryly. Uzun removed the turban and the cowl and placed them on a rock away from the scene. The mullah, now clad only in a long-sleeve white undershirt reaching to his ankles, looked strangely like an obelisk, slim, delicate, and graceful, his long arms flapping in the wind, like a pair of white birds flying around him.

Rahim Khan signaled and the mullah was led toward the gun from where he could see the valley floor alive with thousands of men and women expectantly watching the proceedings. Abolfazl brought a tall stool and placed it under the barrel of the gun and helped the mullah to climb it. Now the wide, black muzzle of the barrel touched the mullah on his back. Standing on another stool to the side, Uzun passed a leather strap from under the mullah's arms, and knotted it tightly around the barrel. Then Abolfazl handed him another strap, which he tied around the barrel, passing it under the arms to the front of the mullah's chest where he secured it with a large knot. He then came down the stool and stood face-to-face with Rahim Khan. The khan paused for a moment. He then nodded to Havar Khan, who stepped forward and sharply kicked the stool from under the mullah. With his arms stretched to his sides, his spindly legs feebly kicking the thin air, his head leaning on his left shoulder, the mullah presented a grotesque sight as he dangled from the barrel of the gun, the muzzle tight against the small of his back. When he opened his eyes, he saw the sea of people on the valley floor rushing to the left and right clearing a path directly in front of him. He closed his eyes.

Rahim Khan, Hajji Ildrum, and Havar Khan moved behind the gun. Rahim Khan reached and softly stroked the wooden trigger of the firing mechanism. He turned to the other two khans and said, "All yours, in the name of God."

"You should do the honors," said Havar Khan, giving a forced chuckle.

Those in attendance tightened the circle around the khans and watched with acute interest the movement of Rahim Khan's thick, rough fingers. Hajji Ildrum stepped back, joining others on the ledge. Rahim Khan then reached for the trigger and jerked it back.

The gun came alive, giving a mighty jolt. The sound of the ensuing explosion shook the hill perceptibly. Those watching the scene all around, fell to their knees, some pressing their foreheads to the ground.

A thick cloud of black smoke emitting from the muzzle of the gun momentarily darkened the sun, and then it was gone.

THE END

Breinigsville, PA USA
13 April 2010
236077BV00001B/8/P